Kiddush Ha-Shem

An Epic of 1648

by Sholom Ash

Translated by Rufus Learsi

PHILADELPHIA:

The Jewish Publication Society of America

5707—1946

60

PRINTED IN THE UNITED STATES OF AMERICA
PRESS OF THE JEWISH PUBLICATION SOCIETY
PHILADELPHIA, PENNA.

To DR. J. L. MAGNES

in token of esteem and affection

"We are ashamed to write down all that the Cossacks and Tatars did unto the Jews, lest we disgrace the species man who is created in the image of God."

—From an old Chronicle.

PART I

CHAPTER ONE

FAR OUT UPON THE STEPPES

Not a thing could be seen. Everything was enveloped in a cloud of smoke which poured right into the room from the oven, where the fire had just been started. Out of the smoke could be heard the small shrill voice of a little boy straining to keep up with the impatient voice of a man. They were chanting a verse from the Pentateuch, the original Hebrew and the Yiddish translation following each other in alternate phrases.

"*Va-yomer*—and He spoke, *Elohim*—God, *el-Moshe*—to Moses, *lemor*—saying."

When the wreaths of smoke grew thinner, there appeared, as through a mist, first the great oven taking up half the room, and on top of it something large, uncouth and shadowy. Soon the thing began to stir, and it seemed as though a portion of the oven was breaking away from the rest. Gradually it assumed the shape of a human being with a huge abdomen and a long red beard. And a massive table appeared through the smoke with numerous barrels and brandy kegs on it, some shelves covered with dry goods, strings of candles hanging from one of them. At the table sat a Jew with curly ear-locks beneath a feather-covered cap. He was wrapped in a sort of woman's quilt-gown kept in place by a scarf and shawl, and was swaying over a large book. On one of the brandy kegs sat a little boy dressed all in white and wrapped in a small prayer-shawl. He was swaying over the Pentateuch in unison with his father, and repeated in his shrill little voice:

"*Va-yomer*—and He spoke, *Elohim*—God, *el Moshe*—to Moses, *lemor*—saying."

But father and son were not permitted to sit long over the Holy Book. From the oven now began to move forward that large, dim, uncouth mass. And only now, when it was quite clear of the oven, was it possible to discern its outlines. It was a tall, stout Greek-Orthodox priest, a massive, staggering figure. His hands were stuck into his broad, red girdle; with a movement of his forehead and without using his hands, he jerked his tall fur hat to the crown of his head. Beads of perspiration broke out on his low forehead, rolled down his hairy nose and disappeared in the endless mazes of his long beard. For a minute he looked blankly at the Jew. Then he said:

"Mendelu, Mendelu, have pity on a Christian soul. Only one more measure, just to drive away the accursed Satan, the evil spirit which torments me to get drunk. I'll put him to sleep and drive him out. Have pity, Mendelu!"

"Ay, ay, Little Father, you will not give that wicked Devil his fill, you will not drive him away. The more you'll pour into his unclean throat, the more he'll torment you. Better not feed him, better let him starve. When the accursed demon will realize that he can expect nothing from you he will leave you, he will enter into Stepan, into Hidrak, but he will leave you."

"Well said! Wisely spoken! You are a man of sense, Mendel, I will obey you," says the large priest, and returns to his place on the wooden bench near the oven and tries to sit still, supporting his massive head in both his hands, and with his long red beard wiping the beads of perspiration from his face.

" *Va-yomer*—and he spake, *Moshe*—Moses, *el b'nai Yisroel*—unto the children of Israel, *lemor*—saying", the Jew resumed his work with the boy.

The priest seized on the word Moses and played with it as he twisted his long red beard.

"Moses, Moshe, Mosè—we know him, we are familiar with him. We've read about him in the Holy Books. He saw God, spoke with God, ascended Mount Sinai,—we know about him. A shepherd he was, a good shepherd to his flock—not like you, Stepan Kratkov," he began to rail at himself, "not like you, in whose fat belly a devil has lodged and torments you. Oh, you thing accursed, you hound's son, you won't be quiet, will you? I'll beat you, beat you out of me! Take this, now!" and the tall priest began to strike with both hands and with all his might at his huge stomach.

"Little Father, dear Little Father, what are you doing? What ails you?" the frightened Jew exclaimed, and his ear-locks began to shake with fear.

"He won't be quiet, the hound's son," the priest points to his stomach, "so I'm going to beat him out."

"Not too hard, gently, gently," the Jew implored, and resumed his occupation with the boy.

Soon, however, the priest again approached the table and, with abashed mien, said to the Jew:

"I beat him but he will not calm down, the hound's son. I'll tell you what, Mendel,—I'll treat him like a good Christian. He torments me and in return I'll give him brandy. I'll treat him with Christian love, that's how I'll fix him. He'll get scared and run away. For wherever Satan feels that Christ is near he avoids that place. Save a soul, dear friend, help carry out a Christian purpose. It's to expel Satan from a sinful belly. Help, Mendel, dear!"

An appeal of that sort the Jew was both unable and afraid to deny. He sighed deeply over the honest penny which he lost through the bargain between Satan and Christian love, a bargain in which he was dragged in against his will. He poured the "little shepherd" a large measure of whiskey, and with even greater energy resumed his swaying over the Pentateuch which lay open before him on the four-fringed garment. And the Little Father took up the holy work of expelling the Devil from his huge stomach with the help of Christian love and Jewish whiskey.

This scene was enacted by the shepherd of the Greek Orthodox flock, Father Stepan, and the Jewish innkeeper Mendel on a snowy winter afternoon in the inn of Zlochov. Zlochov lay far out on the steppe of Podolya, not far from the "green meadow," and belonged to the district squire of Chernin, Konitz-Polski. Mendel was the only Jew who had the courage to hold in lease the inn as well as the Greek Orthodox Church so far out on the steppes near the Zaporozhe Cossacks. Mendel even carried on a trade with the Zaporozhes, and would often go to the Setch on either side of the Dnieper, where the Cossack freemen used to gather to take counsel before waging war on the Turk or for the purpose of choosing their Hetmans. Mendel used to take to the Cossacks calfskin leather, which he obtained from the Jewish tanners of Volhynia, sheepskin coats, flaxen shawls, dyed peasants' wool, fruit brandy and Jewish honey cakes, which Mendel's wife knew so well how to bake and which the Cossacks found so delicious. Sometimes he would come home from the Setch with his beard half plucked or minus one of his ear-locks, but always with his bag full of copper coins, Polish *paims* and *guldens*, pieces of Turkish silver; or he would bring back in barter for his goods Turkish guns and swords with carved ivory handles and studded with precious Oriental stones, Tatar carpets or Cossack cloaks of fox-skin. And Mendel used to take the Cossack goods to the markets of Chihirin and Lubno, where dwelt the Baron Vishnewetzki, the lord of Russ, who was a friend of the Jews and in whose city the Jews were permitted to live and trade freely.

Mendel lived on good terms with his neighbors, the Cossack braves. He kept a little store for them in the inn and he found his income more than ample.

But Mendel felt ill at ease, for he could not live without Jews. And Jews refused to settle in Zlochov, for Zlochov was still an unhallowed spot. It had no synagogue and no Jewish cemetery. All his efforts to secure permission from the nobleman to build a synagogue were of no avail. Father Kozlowski of the Jesuits, who had his seat at Chihirin with the Mission for converting the Cossack peasants to Catholicism, opposed with all his power the granting of permission for a synagogue in Zlochov out of fear lest the Jews turn the Cossacks away from the Catholic faith. And in order to humiliate the Greek Orthodox faith in the eyes of the Cossacks, he forced the innkeeper to hold their church in lease, so that they were compelled to apply to the Jew of the inn for the key to their church.

Mendel made every effort to observe strictly his Jewish faith in that lonely inn in the heart of the steppes among the Cossacks. For the Holy Days he used to go to Chihirin, where he put in "a stock of Judaism" for the entire year.

His only son Shlomo, whom God had vouchsafed to him after his wife, Yocheved, had been childless for six years, and whom, by way of a protecting charm, they still dressed in white, was now a grown boy, six years old, but no Hebrew teacher would come out to the inn. Whatever he knew Mendel taught him himself. But a great deal Mendel himself did not know, and sometimes a ritual question comes up, and the holy books are sealed to him, and the home takes on a certain coarseness. The wife acquires the customs of the Cossack women, and he himself does not know what is permitted and what is not. He has long since been anxious to give up the inn and move into some Jewish settlement, but it is hard to abandon one's livelihood. And so, as far as he was able, he taught Shlomo himself, seated at the table of the inn among the kegs of spirits and the drunkards, as he was doing when he was interrupted by Father Stepan and his Devil, and teaching his little boy all he knew: "*Va-yomer*—and He spake, *Adonai*—God, *el Moshe*—to Moses, *lemor*—saying..."

It would seem, however, that Satan had really been frightened by the Christian love which the priest administered to him. And when the Little Father Stepan was quite drunk, he began to talk like a sober man. He suddenly began to beat his breast with his fist and to rail at himself:

"You are a sinful man, Little Father Stepan. God entrusted you with a flock of little lambs to feed, put the shepherd's crook into your hands: 'take them out to the pasture when they are hungry, and give them to drink when they are thirsty'. But you have not done it. You have not taken them out to pasture when they were hungry, nor have you given them to drink when they were thirsty. Instead, you have sold your soul to the Jew for a measure of spirits. He sits there and prays to his God, while you, Little Father, are guzzling. It's clear, you, my little Jew, have done it. I know it. You have made me drunk while you are praying to God."

"Dear Little Father, what are you saying? What nonsense are you prattling? Go to your church, Little Father,—here, take the key to your church! Pray to your own God, as much as you like,—am I preventing you? On the contrary, a Jew likes to see Christians pray, likes it very much. Here, take the key and go to your church."

"And the keys to the holy church they have turned over to the Jew. They have insulted the church,— insulted the faith, and you, little shepherd, you sit and guzzle. Oh, they will come galloping, the little brothers of the steppes, oh, they will come, those fine lads, on their lightfooted horses, they will come from across the Dnieper and they will avenge the insult to God. They will free the people from the *Pans*, the churches from the Jews, and they will avenge the insult to God."

"Woe is me, what is it I hear? Shh! Hush!" and the Jew ran up from behind the table and covered with his hand the mouth of the priest. "Shh! Hush! The walls will hear it, the winds will carry it to the *Pan*, they will flay you alive—Hush, hush!—" and the Jew looked about him in fear, his ear-locks trembling, lest someone should have heard the priest's words. "Hush! I'll give you brandy—here! Take it and drink! Ah! Father in Heaven, I'm at the end of my strength! That he should have begun in my inn! Why do you punish me so?—A second measure for nothing! Ah, may it give him a disease! Here, drink and be silent!"

Throwing the Jew into a scare with "the little

brothers of the steppe" was the best method of getting whiskey from him after the method of the Devil and Christian love. When the priest had gotten the brimming measure which the Jew, in his great haste, had allowed to run over, he became calm, seated himself again on the bench of the oven, and, twisting with his hands his long, red beard, he took a sip every now and then. And the Jew returned to his place behind the table, but was unable to go on with his teaching. He groaned again and again.

"Dear Father in Heaven, why do you punish me so? Wherein have I sinned? If I refuse to hold the church in lease, I catch it from the Polish Jesuit; if I do hold the church in lease, this one scares me with his little brothers. And a synagogue is not allowed, and Jews are not to be found, and learning I have none, and the son is growing up without Torah! I'll give up this inn! I'll run away from Zlochov, I'll run wherever my legs will carry me! Without a synagogue and without Jews—only drunken priests! Ah! woe is me!"

"Don't you run away, Mendelu,—don't you forsake us, Mendelu," rejoined the priest who, to all appearances, had not paid any heed to the words of the Jew. "You are like a good little father to us; and as for a synagogue, we'll give you one. The little brothers will come from the steppe, they will come on their lightfooted horses, will kill all the *Pans* and give you a synagogue. I'll intercede for you."

"Help, help! He is beginning again with the little brothers! Hush, be silent, hush!" And again the Jew ran out from behind the table in great fear.

Who knows how the matter would have ended if old Marusha, an old strong Cossack woman who was in service at the Jew's, had not come to his aid in his hour of need. She came in from the next house, which was fenced off from the inn where the Jew lived, and took her stand in front of the priest with her arms, thick, muscular, and naked in the cold winter day, akimbo.

"It's necessary, Little Father, to beat you up a little for your own good," said the old woman, "otherwise you'll not calm down. You have made the Devil groggy and now some demon speaks out of you."

"Help, mother dear, help! Do a Christian deed. I have beaten him, but he pays no attention to me. He is on too familiar terms with me, the Devil."

"Wait, dear Little Father, wait, I'll help you." And she took the slop-pail which stood near the door of the inn and spilled the contents over the head of the priest.

"Ah! How good!" the priest spluttered with delight.

"How now, Little Father, you feel better?" asked Marusha.

"He needs to be beaten a little more, then he'll quiet down altogether."

"Wait, Little Father, wait, I'll help you." And old Marusha went up to the priest, and with her two large, powerful fists she belabored his stomach.

"Easy now! not so hard! Gently, gently!" the Jew gesticulated from a distance.

CHAPTER TWO

LOSING COUNT OF THE DAYS

Twilight began to filter in. The snow beneath the windows took on a reddish hue which soon became purple. The wind of the steppe beat upon the walls of the inn and behaved as though it would lift the straw roof of the house if it were not admitted. The inn became dark. The priest, after Marusha had driven the demon out of him, fell asleep on the bench in front of the oven. His snoring sounded like the blasts of a shepherd's horn, and confused all who were in the room.

The innkeeper's wife, Yocheved, entered from the next room, which was separated by a thin partition wall. She had a piece of burning kindling wood in her hand which lighted up her young fresh face and the head-dress and shawls which she wore. She approached the oven and lighted a wick which was floating in a large vessel filled with melted wax. She lifted a large wooden bowl and began to pour into it flour for kneading dough.

"What are you doing, Yocheved?" Mendel asked.

"Kneading dough for the Sabbath bread. The oven is already warm."

"Sabbath bread in the middle of the week?"

"Woe is me, it is Thursday today," the woman answered in a tone of surprise.

"Yocheved, you are making a mistake; it is only Wednesday. Have you lost the count again, Yocheved?" the man cried. "Yocheved, we are living in a wilderness where there are no Jews, and you lose count of the days."

The woman stood with the burning stick of wood in her hand in a guilty attitude, and she said imploringly:

"You are taking my heart out, Mendel. Look into the calendar. Why, it is Thursday today, Mendel."

Mendel groaned and approached the large cardboard which hung on the wall of the inn,—the calendar which the Assembly of the Four Countries had published in Lublin for the use of the innkeepers in the outlying provinces. The calendar was underlined in different colors, and little wooden pegs were stuck into it which served as different symbols that Mendel had devised for himself. For a very long time Mendel contemplated the calendar, then he asked his wife:

"Yocheved, what day was the day before yesterday, Monday or Tuesday?"

"Woe is me, you don't know what day it was day before yesterday? Mendel, Mendel, Mendel, if you don't know, how am I to know, who am only a sinful woman?"

Mendel again contemplated the calendar, while Yocheved stood near in agony. Her husband's forgetting the day had the same effect on her as if she had lost her way in the steppe all alone and at night.

"Mendel, what are we going to do? Mendel, is it not a dreadful thing that a Jew should not know what day of the week it is?"

"Why do you cry? Why do you shout? Call in Marusha."

Marusha, the Cossack woman who served in the house of Mendel, had become so expert in Jewish customs and religious duties in the course of the years that she had spent with Yocheved, that one of her functions was to look after the religious observances of the home. With Shlomele, Mendel's only son whom she had nursed and raised, she said the morning and evening prayers regularly. She reminded him to say the benedictions over his food at every meal. Marusha was also required to remember the day of the week so that they might know when to prepare for the Sabbath.

Hearing the loud cries of her master and mistress, Marusha entered and, upon learning that they were confused in the calendar and did not know when to prepare for the Sabbath, she was so frightened that although she knew that the day before yesterday was Monday, she became bewildered and was afraid to say anything decisive in so important a matter.

"How should I know, mistress, I am only a Christian soul. It was either Monday or it was Tuesday. Oh Lord, have mercy."

Husband and wife looked at each other in alarm. All of them, the man, the woman and the servant, began to shout at once, and the boy, hearing the grown-ups shout, began to cry. The noise awakened the sleeping priest. He yawned several times and looked around in surprise.

"Dear Little Father, save us," Mendel implored him. "Do you not know what day we had day before yesterday? Was it Monday or Tuesday?"

"Monday—Tuesday—day before yesterday—. Wait, let me see," said the priest, rolling up his sleeves and beginning to reckon on his fingers. "Saint George's day is always on a Thursday, the first day after the second week after Saint Paul's day when it begins to snow. That's the time we say a special prayer in church for the holy Saint Anthony."

"Woe is me, the priest has become your teacher. Mendel, Mendel!" and the woman began to weep.

Mendel turned again to the calendar, but his search was in vain. In order to know if it was Wednesday or Thursday he would have to know what the day before yesterday was, whether Monday or Tuesday, and there was not a living soul in Zlochov who could tell him that.

For a minute the entire household was reduced to fear and terror. They were afraid to stir as if waiting for the world to come to an end. But suddenly the door opened and, driven by the clattering wind, there stumbled into the inn a short, snow-covered creature, wrapped in an overcoat, shawls, scarves and all sorts of clothes. No human face was visible. So entirely covered with snow was the figure that it looked like a snowball. But by the

voice which made itself heard, it was to be perceived
that it was a human creature.

"Blessed be God, does a Jew live here?" said
the voice.

"A Jew, a Jew," answered the man, the woman,
the servant, and even the priest, with immense joy,
gathering around the short, snow-covered individual.
The little snow-man began to peel off the snow-covered
scarves, shawls and coats one after another and, after
he had thrown aside his various garments, there
remained standing a slight, short Jew with snow-white
hair, a short white beard, a pair of brilliant child-
like eyes and a smile which was wise and child-like
at the same time. He held out a hand of greeting
to Mendel.

"Blessed be God, I have stumbled upon a Jew.
Sholom aleichem!"

"Come close to the oven, friend, it is lighted," said
the innkeeper's wife.

The little Jew approached the oven and embraced
it as one embraces a good old friend and said:

"To think a Jew would go to live so far out in the
steppe! Ah, Lord of the Universe, what places
your Jews seek you out in! Way out in the steppe
they seek you out, Father in Heaven."

"Whence have you roamed to this distant place?"
Mendel at last thought of asking.

"From nowhere in particular. I am, you see, a
jolly little tailor, well known, thank God, in these
parts among the renters. I sew sheepskin coats
and garments for the little ones, may they wear

them in good health, trousseaus for weddings and
such other things that Jews need. When I heard
in Karsoon that Zlochov already has a Jewish innkeeper, I thought to myself, I will take a trip down
and find out how a Jew is getting along in such a
far away place. And at the same time I might come
upon a garment to sew over, or some children to
teach, for, you see, I'm a teacher also, with the help
of God."

"As if God Himself had brought you at just the
right moment. We have forgotten what day of
the week it is. Living among *goyim* all alone in
the wilderness, we have lost count of the day", says
the woman. "Do you not know, friend, what day
of the week we Jews have today?"

"Forgotten the day? My, my! What need has
a Jew for knowing the day of the week in a wilderness?
On account of the Sabbath, I suppose, to know when
to knead the dough for the white Sabbath bread.
See, dear Father, how faithful Your Jews are to You
even in the wild steppe. Among *goyim* they forget
You not, they observe Your Sabbath, and are deeply
grieved when they forget the day of the week. I
will let you know it, and soon. Let me only look
at my knots." And the little Jew takes up the cord
of his pack. "It happens often that I too forget
the day, so I make these signs. Every day I make
a knot in the cord of my pack. My knots tell me
that today we have,—let me see—yes! the fourth
day of the week,—Wednesday, for all Jews! And
here let me give you some good advice. Lay up

pieces of wood on the oven for a sign as other renters
are doing. On Sunday you put one piece of wood
on the oven, Monday another, Tuesday still another,
and when you count seven pieces of wood you know
that the holy Sabbath has come. And that is done
by the woman of the house," he turned to Yocheved,
"because it is dangerous to depend on the man."

"Many thanks for the good advice you give us,"
says Mendel on behalf of his bashful wife. "Now
go and prepare some barley soup for our guest."
And turning to the latter he said:

"Until my wife will have the barley ready we will
say the evening prayer. It is getting late."

The inn was now transformed into a synagogue.
In one corner stood the father with his son, in the
other the guest, and they pronounced the Eighteen
Benedictions together.

From the oven came the odor of the barley-soup
which Yocheved seasoned with an onion. The odor
pervaded the room and teased the appetite of the big
priest. He inhaled it through his big nostrils, swallowed
his saliva and smacked his lips. He knew, however,
that his prospects for sharing in the plate of barley
soup were slim and he became very sad. He rubbed
his back against the oven and, licking his lips like
a kitten, he said to himself with great self-pity:

"Ah, dear Father, dear God, the blasphemous
Jews are eating barley-soup with sliced onions, and a
pious Christian soul has to starve. Avenge yourself,
dear Father, dear God!"

Mendel pretended not to notice the glowing eyes

of the overheated, red-faced priest. He invited his guest into the next room and posted Marusha behind the table of the inn to stand guard over the barrels and flasks of brandy. And the priest groaned bitterly on seeing Marusha with her bare arms standing behind the table. All his hopes vanished and he strove to give himself over to pious thoughts.

During the meal, while the guest was enveloped in the vapor which rose from the earthenware dish of barley-soup in the center of the table, he examined the boy. Pinching Shlomele's cheek, he asked:

"Well, tell me, big fellow, what are you learning now?"

"Six years old already, praise God," his father answers for him, "and he has only begun the Bible. It is hard being a Jew in the steppe."

"God will compensate you," the guest consoles him. "You will some day have the privilege of seeing Zlochov a Jewish settlement, and you will live to be the Parnas of the community."

Mendel was thoughtful a while.

"And the place really needs a synagogue," the guest added. "Such a large, broad steppe and without a synagogue. And if the Lord of the Universe wants His Jews to pray to Him, the nobleman will have to grant the synagogue. He will have to, he will be compelled to. Heaven itself will compel him. Is it possible for him to oppose it?"

CHAPTER THREE

A Synagogue! A Synagogue!

The Lord Konitz-Polski came down to Zlochov for the hunt, and in his hunting-lodge he arranged a ball for his guests. The steward of Zlochov sent Mendel to Nemirov for a Jewish band of musicians and a supply of gloves, which Mendel was to sell to "their Excellencies" for dancing with the noble Polish ladies.

The hunting-lodge was built with high towers in the Swedish style, and the halls were lighted by numerous candles in iron chandeliers. And the Polish gentlemen in long capes with broad sable collars hanging down their shoulders, holding in their hands their Hussar caps decorated with peacock feathers, led to the Mazurka the noble ladies who were dressed in white satin trimmed with royal ermine. The Jewish fiddle quavered, scraping out long-drawn tunes, and the Jewish cymbals of the Nemirov band beat sweetly and resonantly to the measure. Their "Exalted Excellencies" beat time to the music with the pointed bronze spurs of their heels, and the ladies also beat time with the golden little heels with which their fur boots were ornamented, and Mendel ran about with new-pressed gloves from one gallant to another, saying beseechingly:

"A pair of gloves for the dance with the beautiful and radiant noble lady."

After each dance the gallants threw away their gloves and snatched up a new pair from Mendel. It was not proper to use the same pair with the new partner. Mendel's little boy, Shlomele, with the trembling ear-locks, went in and out between the legs of the gentlemen, collected the gloves which had been thrown away and brought them to his father. The latter put them into the wooden press, made them smooth and peddled them again among the cavaliers.

"Change your gloves, Excellencies,—in honor of the ladies, change your gloves. It is not proper to dance with the radiant noble ladies in used gloves, Excellencies."

Mendel did not rest a minute. When he was not selling the gloves, he pressed them, singing at the same time verses from the Psalms, which he knew by heart, and spacing them with sighs and groans.

"Ah, how the Gentiles rejoice—my calamities on them, my wife's travailing ills and my child's tooth-ache and measles and fever, dear Father in Heaven. Gross materialists they are, gluttons and drunkards and idol worshippers. And a synagogue, a holy synagogue they will not permit to be built. Is it not time that Thou shouldst rebuild Thy Holy Temple? Well, I suppose the time is not yet, so let it be as is pleasing unto Thee, Father in Heaven!"

"Hey, there, Jew! stop mumbling your devilish prayer. You are going to bring the devil down upon us! Let me have gloves for the Mazurka with the noble little lady of Zlochov, the radiant and adorable Mademoiselle Sophie, whose little head is like a white dove,—but not the pressed ones which your little bastard is picking up from under the feet of the dancers—bright and new they must be for the delicately shaped waist of my dove-headed angel."

"What is your Exalted Excellency saying? Who am I that would dare to defraud so Exalted an Excellency like yourself? Why, I even knew your father, the noble old gentleman. Ah, what a good nobleman he was!" And in Hebrew he added: "Thus perish all the wicked."

"What cursed thing is that which you said in your devil's language? I will flay you alive if you will curse my father in his grave."

"I blessed your father, blessed him in our holy language before our God, that he may dwell in our beautiful Heaven."

"Bless not and curse not, Jew. Have a care for your skin and hide beneath your wife's skirts when I set my dogs on you. Faster, Jew, faster, hurry now, my feet are on edge for the dance."

"One more minute, Excellency. Let them stay in the press another minute. The longer they are in the press the cleaner and the firmer do they become. Just like a human being, Excellency. Just like us Jews, Excellency."

At this point there approached the proprietor of Zlochov, the Lord Konitz-Polski, tall, broadshouldered and powerful, like a great oak tree.

His long black satin coat, which reached down to
his feet, made his body appear even more powerful,
and he looked as though he had been carved out of
wood, like a huge stump, except that from his broad
shoulders emerged, like a tower on a roof, his long
pointed head with shaved ear-locks and crown.   His
big, thick mustaches, like those of a powerful catfish,
ran from ear to ear.

"Listen, Jew, you will entertain my guests tonight
with one of the songs which you sing. If you will
sing well, you will be able to obtain something from
me, understand?"

"I understand, Exalted Excellency."

The Jew sprang backwards from the nobleman and
called his little son, who was still engaged in picking
up the discarded gloves from under the feet of the
dancers. His father smoothed out his ear-locks and
stationed him near himself. The gentlemen and
noble ladies began to gather round the Jew and the
little boy. The hall became silent, the musicians
stopped playing, only the burning candles sputtered
from time to time, and from the distant corners and
neighboring rooms could be heard the muffled laughter
and twitter of the radiant blond maidens and love-
sick "Excellencies".

The preparations lasted a long time. Suddenly
the Jew became completely transformed. He closed
his eyes and his face flushed red.   It was clear that
he was struggling to transport himself, to attain
some other region. And suddenly he succeeded.
With a quick movement he put one of his fingers under

his chin and all at once began to sing. At first he sang slowly and softly, as though humming to himself, but soon his singing became louder, his voice acquired daring. The Jew lost consciousness of his surroundings. The nobles laughed a moment longer, but soon they were completely silent. It appeared as if the Jew were the sole master of that vast hall. He saw neither the gentlemen nor the ladies nor the glitter of satin and furs which surrounded him. No one was there but he alone—he and his betrothed. And it was no mortal woman to whom he now intoned his great song of praise, but a higher, a spiritual being. It was his Sabbath, his Mother, to whom he sang; he sang to his hopes, to his tribulations:

"A woman of valor who can find?"

No serenade to an earthly mistress did he sing, but a serenade to his heavenly mistress, to the invisible and ineffable bliss which she grants to him who thinks of her. He sang of the great holiness and purity which emanate from her and make beautiful those who think of her and love her. Of his Bride the Sabbath he sang, of his only Bride of thousands of years, and of the great and everlasting love which his children's children unto the last generation will feel for the Eternal Bride. The misfortunes and humiliations which he bears for her sake became transformed into honor and glory, the life of a dog was changed into the life of a prince. Through the love which is borne her, she transforms all things into heavenly bliss. Of what importance then were his neighbors and the nobles with their puny possessions, with their tiny bit of earthly happiness, with their vain and evanescent human strength and power, compared to the eternity of his love for his magnificent Bride?

The nobles were silenced and abashed in the presence of the mighty nobleman standing in their midst and singing a song of eternal love.

"You have served me well! You have sung well, and my guests are pleased, Jew. Say what you wish. Ask for a great deal, and don't be too long about it. I am more afraid of your craftiness than of your appetite," the Pan laughed.

"Exalted Excellency," the Jew threw himself at the feet of the noble, "a synagogue and a cemetery! A synagogue for prayer, and a cemetery for burying our dead. Give us permission to have a synagogue and a cemetery in Zlochov."

The squire fell to thinking for a minute. He remembered the pearls which Zechariah of Chihirin brought him when he came to that city. Zlochov would likewise become a considerable settlement and would pay taxes, but how would God and Father Kozlowski like it? But an idea promptly occurred to him which would serve the double purpose of insuring good taxes and guaranteeing that God would be pleased.

"If you will bow your head three times before our Lord Jesus Christ and pronounce the Benediction before Holy Mary three times, I will grant the permission and give you a handsome site for a cemetery."

The Jew remained silent, and as though stunned.

"Well, Jew, shall we settle the affair? You need only say, 'Mary, Holiest Mother of God, be Thou praised for ever and ever, Amen.'"

The Jew remained silent.

"Well, Jew, kneel but before her."

The Jew was still silent.

"Then you will have to play the bear."

The Jew turned pale and began to stammer.

"Exalted Excellency, I am only a poor Jew. Have pity on my wife, on my little children. Pray, Shlomele, my little boy, pray to the noble lord. Have pity, Exalted Excellency, I will always serve you faithfully."

And father and child embraced the squire's feet and kissed his boots and the floor in front of him, and beat the floor with their foreheads.

"Have pity on the little orphans, Exalted Excellency."

"Either pronounce the Benediction or play the bear."

The Jew thought a while. He was pale and frightened, and kept repeating verses from the Psalms and the prayers, kissing the coat and boots of the noble. But suddenly he saw light. His hands and knees still trembled, but his face was now calm and tranquil.

"For a synagogue, Exalted Excellency. Have pity. God will help. Do as you will."

The noble motioned with his head, and two servants took the Jew and pulled over him the skin of a bear. The noble then ordered the musicians to

play, and the two servants began to lash the bear
with long whips. The bear jumped about, growling:
"Brr, brr!"

The noble gentlemen writhed with laughter and
pushed one another towards the bear, and the servants lashed and chased him from place to place.
The Jew behind the bearskin growled:

"The Lord is my light and my salvation; whom
shall I fear?—Brr, brr!" And he sprang on all
fours from place to place. "The Lord is the strong-
hold of my life; of whom shall I be afraid?"

"You have played the bear well, Jew. You shall
have the synagogue for it; the cemetery you are still
to earn."

Breathless the Jew ran home from the hunting-
lodge, his long four-fringed prayer-shawl getting
tangled between his legs. The little boy with the
trembling ear-locks ran after him, and from the other
side of the road both cried out, bringing the good
tidings to the mother:

"A synagogue! A synagogue!"

CHAPTER FOUR

THE DEDICATION OF THE SYNAGOGUE

Promptly it became known throughout Podolya and Volhynia, wherever Jews were to be found, that a new Jewish settlement had been established. Zlochov having obtained permission to build a synagogue, Jews from all the surrounding districts began to move into that town. There came Jews from Kherson, from Chihirin, from the other side of the Dnieper, from Lubno, from Lachovitch and from Preyaslaw. For the reports stated further that Zlochov was a good place for making a living. It was not far from the *Setch*, and it was possible to carry on trade with the Cossacks; and Jews came even from Little Poland who, at the annual fairs which were held in Yarislaw and Lublin, had heard that Zlochov had become a Jewish settlement.

First of all the Jews set to work building the synagogue. They contributed towards the common fund whatever they could, the women offering their jewels. Two Jewish master builders were brought down from Nemirov and commissioned to build the synagogue.

It took two years to build it. The townspeople themselves took a hand in the actual building. The synagogue had to serve two purposes: as a house of prayer and as a place of defense against enemies.

The synagogue was therefore built like a fort with iron doors and bolts. Nachman the blacksmith, who ran the town smithy, fashioned the iron door for the synagogue, the railing for the central platform, a large menorah for the pulpit-stand and a large Chanukkah lamp. His work was simple and rough, but performed with great love and diligence. All the artifices of which Nachman was capable he lavished on the railing for the central platform, on the Menorah and on the Chanukkah lamp. The same was done by Boruch the carpenter. Under the supervision of the two master builders from Nemirov he carved various figures and designs which he remembered from the days of his apprenticeship, pigeons and other birds, stags and lions, the symbols of the twelve tribes and the signs of the Zodiac. Through long nights he sat by the light of a burning stick of wood, carving the woodwork for the synagogue. And when the head of a household went to the annual fair in one of the large cities and saw an attractive object, a fine piece of silk for an ark-curtain, a biblical scene to hang on the east wall, a fancy chair in honor of the prophet Elijah or some other ornament, he bought it and took it home for the synagogue. And the women sat up through the winter nights in the inn with Mendel's wife and, singing pious songs, sewed their jewels into the curtains for the Ark and into the covers for the scrolls of the Torah.

Mendel, as the first settler of Zlochov, enjoying as he did the confidence of the Polish proprietor, became the parnas of the new community and, anxious

that Zlochov should acquire some standing in the
world, he decided to secure as rabbi some great scholar
with a big reputation.

The community at Lachovitch had a rabbi who
was surnamed the "Gate of Justice", and whose praises
were sung loud throughout the region. Mendel
made up his mind quickly, harnessed a wagon, pro-
ceeded to Lachovitch, offered the rabbi twelve Polish
pence a week more than Lachovitch gave, and granted,
moreover, to the rabbi's wife a monopoly in providing
the town with candles. He thus obtained the rabbi's
consent together with a written promise. Later,
when Lachovitch became aware of the matter, it
was already too late. Mendel took the Gaon of
Lachovitch to Zlochov, and in this way Zlochov at
once acquired a name in the world. The rabbi
organized classes, looked after the Hebrew schools,
taught the young men Talmud, so that Zlochov began to be a place of learning.

And when it got to be known at the fairs of Yarislaw and Lublin that Zlochov had become a place
of learning, there began to arrive in the new settlement not only artisans and merchants but also scholars
and men of refinement. Reb Jacob Cohen came
to Zlochov from a small town in Germany which had
been destroyed following a blood accusation, only
Reb Jacob, fleeing with the Torah scrolls of the
town, escaping. And another was Reb Israel of
Bohemia, who came to Zlochov with his little daughter
from the town of Asch. They had heard at the annual
fair in Lublin that in the distant regions of the steppe

God had permitted settlements where Jews could find a livelihood, and so they came down to settle in Zlochov.

And Mendel was anxious to bring about a union between his family and one of high pedigree, since Shlomele was already eight years old, and it was time to think of getting him married, in order, in this manner, to hasten the end of the Exile. And Mendel the parnas desired to ally himself with the "Gate of Justice", who had a little girl of Shlomele's age, so he promised maintenance to the couple all his life-time and a large number of gold coins. And in order to dedicate the synagogue, as was the custom, with a wedding of the first families of the town, the marriage ceremony was postponed until the day of dedication. The children, it is true, were still young, but this was done so as to grant them the privilege of dedicating the synagogue with their marriage.

The synagogue was ready for Passover, but the dedication was postponed until Lag B'Omer, for that day is considered to be very lucky.

Outside the synagogue looked small, that it might not be conspicuous in the eyes of the Gentiles, but inside it was high and wide. The floor was dug deep into the ground, twelve steps beneath the level of the entrance, and it sloped down even deeper so that the pulpit-stand where the cantor stood was the lowest spot of all. This was done for two reasons: in the first place, so that the synagogue should not loom big in the eyes of the Gentiles and, secondly, when prayers were offered to God, it would be done in accordance with the verse in the Psalms: "Out of the depths I have called Thee, Oh Lord." But from the pulpit-stand there were carved steps which led up to the Ark, for it is not fitting that the Word of God should be lodged in the depths.

On this day the Ark was draped in the new festive curtain, which was embroidered with silver threads on blue Florentine brocade. The crown of the Torah shone down from the curtain with the subdued Sabbath glow of the chaste pearls which used to lend so much grace to the pure white throats of the young Jewish matrons at the time of blessing the Sabbath candles. Those pearls were hallowed with the tranquil charm of Sabbath evenings. And deep-red rubies sparkled like red wine out of the clusters of grapes which hung on green branches made of emeralds. The names of the pious women and maidens were embroidered on the curtain, as well as their prayers, prayers for virtuous children and sweet hopes and modest and chaste longings for love. Thus did that little curtain exhale a feminine charm bestowed by the delicate fingers of women, and suggesting the chaste music which is heard issuing from Jewish houses on Sabbath nights.

In the center of the synagogue stood the platform built of hard chestnut wood and carved with the names of the twelve tribes and their standards. Each tribe had its own flag and color. Judah, as the king, was brilliant with gold, with the lion at his feet; Simeon with his captured city of Shechem,

where rose up the walls and towers of that city which
he had conquered to avenge the shame of his sister;
and the ship of Zebulun floated in a sea of silver;
the blossoming tree, the symbol of Asher, was studded
with green stones; out of copper was fashioned the
serpent of Dan. And above the platform hung a
canopy like the deep blue sky of the evening in which
golden stars twinkled and the twelve signs of the
Zodiac floated in the blue night, each over its cor-
responding tribe. On the platform there now stood
the leading men with the scrolls of the Torah in their
arms, ready to place them in the new dwelling which
they had built for the glory of God. Among them
stands Reb Jacob Cohen from Germany, and the
scroll which he holds is the only thing left to him of
his numerous family and of the entire community
which was scattered and dispersed to the four corners of the earth. And there stands Reb Israel with
the scroll of the synagogue of the city of Asch.
During the panic he had become separated from his
wife and children, so he had come to Poland to look
for them. For he had been told that many Jews
from Bohemia had saved themselves in Poland. He
had wandered from one fair to another until he came
to Zlochov with his child, and settled there.

And among these old worthies, rich with tribulations
and tested in the fires of martyrdom, with the scrolls
of the devastated communities in their arms, stood
the new leader, the parnas of the community, Reb
Mendel, with a new scroll which had been written
at his behest for the new community of Zlochov.

The new scroll has as yet no covering stained with
the blood of martyrs and with the tears of fugitives.
Its covering is still new and unstained, and its guardian
Mendel, still looks strong and untried. His face is
without the holy glow imparted by sorrow and suffering and self-sacrifice; no trace, as yet, of that nobility
which proceeds from the readiness for the supreme
sacrifice. But with his large and heavy hands he
clasps the new scroll of the Torah very tightly.
There is fear in his heart because of the sacred burden which he has assumed to be the parnas of a
community. He realizes how great and holy is the
burden which is borne by the old parnasim, the
leaders of the ruined communities among whom he
now stands. And his heart beats fast. Will the
time ever come when he, too, will have to stand by
his community and his Torah, even as they had done,
at the risk of his life? Will he be ready for the
supreme sacrifice for the sanctification of His Name,
even as they were? Will not his heart become faint?
Is he worthy of the honor and the obligation which
he has assumed?

Suddenly the entire assemblage became silent.
A holy stillness reigned throughout the synagogue
as though some one invisible had entered. Reb
Jacob took up his scroll of the Torah, lifted it on high
and, in a voice full of tears, began to intone the prayer
of gratitude of those who have been saved from great
danger, thanking God who had rescued him from all
perils and brought him, together with his scroll,
to a place of safety. A subdued sobbing was heard

from the women's section below. It was the wife
of one of the exiles who remembered her dear ones,
from whom she had become separated. The weeping
affected the entire congregation. They were seized
with a dread of the days to come: Will they, too,
ever have to abandon their synagogue, even as Reb
Jacob had done, the synagogue which they had built
with so much labor and love, and take their scrolls
and go? Who can say what things are hidden in
the lap of the days to come?   And one after another the exiles intoned the prayer of the rescued.
And when the young cantor, whom Reb Mendel had
brought from Uman, began in his guttural voice
to pronounce the names of those who had given their
lives for the sanctification of His Name, the weeping
became universal. From all eyes the tears flowed
silently, and a prayer to God rose up from the depths
of every heart, that the little synagogue might be
their final place of rest and refuge until the coming
of the Messiah.

"God grant that this be our last exile," the Jews
wished each other.

"And may we be preserved from all evil." The
women kissed each other and wept.

Soon, however, the sorrowful mood departed, and
the faces of young and old lighted up like a rain-
covered field on which the sun is shining. It was
the singing of the cantor, accompanied by Isaac
Aaron's playing on the violin, which lighted up every
saddened countenance. The cantor was singing
the portion prior to the opening of the Ark.

And Shlomele, Mendel's son, dressed in a coat of green silk which the little tailor, his teacher, had made him for his wedding, opened the Ark. One after another the men mounted the steps and placed the scrolls of the Torah into the new Ark. Two lions of wood with crowns on their heads stood one on each side of the Ark guarding the scrolls, and two large gilt eagles flew down, by means of a secret mechanism which the woodturner of Nemirov had invented, from the heights where they had rested beneath the starry blue sky, and remained suspended over the Ark, protecting the scrolls with their broad wings. First honors were given to the scrolls of the exiles. First came old Reb Jacob with his scroll. Then followed Reb Israel of Germany, and then the rabbi of the synagogue. Last of all came Mendel with the new scroll of the community of Zlochov. And when his turn came to put his unadorned scroll into the Ark, he remained standing a minute before it and his heart was filled with a silent prayer: "Dear Father in Heaven, may it be a resting place for our children and children's children," and a tear, the first tear, fell from the eyes of the new parnas upon the robe of the Torah scroll.

Soon the violin began to play, the drum beat to measure and a choir of little singers with thin little voices began to sing: "Lord who Fillest the Universe." The congregation took up the song, and with it their joy waxed ever greater. The sad mood vanished as well as the dread which had reigned before. The joyous fervor of Jewish worship filled the

Synagogue, and seized upon the people. The voices of the little choir boys tinkled like little bells around the necks of goats that are being taken to graze in green pastures.

And now the violins broke into the singing like a rush of fountains. They began to play the wedding music. The little tailor, Shlomele's teacher, made sexton of the synagogue, now came in, dressed in broad Polish trousers of the color of wool, which he had sewed for himself for the wedding, skipping with the canopy-poles in his hands and crying half in Yiddish, half in Polish:

"Ho there, Jews, stand aside, don't you see who is coming? It is Pan Itzik coming to the wedding!"

The boys and young men took hold of the canopy-poles and set up the canopy on the platform. A flute was heard as if heralding the approach of a lord, and suddenly there broke upon the scene a red and golden shimmer and glittering of pearls and diamonds on the breasts of women, and tufts of feathers and jewels on headdresses. There was a sparkle of red silk from Slutzk interwoven with threads of gold, a crimson glow of blood-red beads in the midst of starry strings of pearls, and yellow agate bloomed like golden-yellow flowers on white satin. Delicate, white lace-points rose like the foam of the sea on the breasts of the women. Heavy, gold-embroidered scarfs wound over the silk as though anxious to guard the mysterious loveliness of feminine charms. Slowly and with dignified gait walked the mothers in all their pomp and splendor, leading the bride between them. She was still a little child, not yet ten years old, nevertheless she was needed in order "to hasten the coming of the Messiah." Her black curls had fallen beneath the shears, and as the child did not know that her soul was required for the salvation of the world, she had protested and had not permitted her black locks to fall until Leah, the bath-attendant, had paid her with sweet cookies, a cooky for each lock. Even now her road to the canopy is sweetened by the sugar cookies which she had purchased with her locks... She was dressed in the wedding-robe of gold cloth which the community had ordered. This coat was intended to be worn by every bride who was led to the canopy in order not to cause the poor to be ashamed who had no silk dresses of their own. For the first time she was wearing the wedding-dress, and after her all the brides of Zlochov would wear it when going to the canopy. And all the maidens of Zlochov, holding lighted tapers, twisted and colored brilliant Polish ribbons, illumined the road to the canopy of the first bride of Zlochov.

Now the bride is already beneath the canopy and playing with the flounces of her dress, but the bride-groom is not there yet. The wedding bard has already sung his ballad, the musicians have played their "piece", and the bridegroom is not yet in sight. In vain the sexton and the trustees are running about with lighted candles, looking in all the corners for the bridegroom. At last he was found hiding underneath the chair of the prophet Elijah. He was be-

trayed by his long, green, silken coat, and his teacher
chased him from beneath the chair with his stick:

"Bridegroom, to the canopy with you!"

But the little fellow kicked hard with his new spiked
boots, and refused to come out from under the chair
until his father pulled him out by his ear-locks.

He was ashamed before his playmates, who stuck
out their tongues behind him and sang in his ears
the following rhyme:

All the folks are gaily dancing,
Laughing, singing, skipping, prancing,
Shlomele still weeps and weeps.
Shlomele, Shlomele, why dost weep?
Why, I weep, ah well I know
Neath the canopy I must go.

He kicked with his heavy boots, but he went to
the canopy, his father dragging him by his ear.
They were afraid that he might run away from beneath the canopy, so his father held him by the coat
on one side and his teacher on the other. He, therefore, vented his wrath on the bride, digging her in
the ribs until she won him over with one of the cookies
which she had purchased with her locks. Then
he consented to the match.

And far and wide pealed the song of the new synagogue over the desert steppes of Ukraine, and the
message was borne over field and forest, and every
tree and every blade of grass whispered in the warm
spring night: "A synagogue has been built, a
marriage consecrated, God's blessing is at hand!
God's blessing is at hand!"

CHAPTER FIVE

THE MARRIED COUPLE

It cannot be said that the young couple, Shlomele and Deborah, lived on very friendly terms after the wedding. And to Shlomele's shame it must be said that it was he who was always at fault whenever the domestic peace was disturbed. Shlomele, who was then thirteen years old and preparing for *bar mizvah* (confirmation), was attending the class of the Talmud teacher, and felt thoroughly at home in the great sea of the Talmud, conversant with all the laws of marriage, with the details of marriage contracts and with all the obligations which a wife owes to her husband and a husband to his wife. He was also familiar with all the laws of divorce. Shlomele, who knew how to unite two opposites by means of an adroit interpretation of a text, and could build up "towers of Babel" by means of a *pilpul*, was often the recipient of a flogging at the hands of his teacher. The latter was very little impressed by the important position which Shlomele occupied in the world as a married man. The husband would then avenge himself for the lashes of his teacher on the head-dress of his little wife. Finding his wife seated near the threshhold of the inn, playing in the sand, he would snatch the head-dress from her head and fill it with sand.

"There, that's what you get for having mocked at me."

"For this they will flog you in hell with burning lashes," his little wife warned him.

"The sin is yours for standing under the sky without a covering for your head."

Then the wife declared their relations severed in the following terms:

> Shlomele, Shlomele, don't speak to me,
> Blind your eyes and never see;
> Filled with blood little buckets two,
> Never will I speak to you.
> 'Mong little buckets filled with chalk
> Will I never with you walk.

Thereupon the young man accepted her declaration and turned on his heel. And his wife covered her eyes with both her hands so as not to see him.

It is a Friday afternoon in the summer. The inn is full of Russian peasants and Polish Pans. Mendel is busy in the inn with the drygoods and the brandy, Yocheved with preparing for the Sabbath, and outside the children are engaged in a loud quarrel. Hearing the great noise, Marusha stepped out and, seeing what Shlomele had done with his little wife's head-dress, she began to scold him.

"Rascal that you are, is that the way to treat a wife? You should be fond of her, not throw sand on her head."

"Ha, ha", the young man stuck out his tongue at her. "You are of the lineage of Balaam's ass, and you will have no portion in the world to come, and your soul will enter into a dog and a cat, because you are not descended from Father Jacob but from the wicked Esau."

"It is you who are descended from the wicked Esau. You are an Esau yourself," the servant scolded him. "You have committed a sin, letting your wife stand outdoors with uncovered head. Is that permitted? For that they will burn and roast you in hell." Thus the Christian servant took up the little wife's grievance.

Shlomele remembered that he had not yet been given the pudding to which he is entitled on Fridays. He demanded it.

"Give me the pudding, and have done!"

"You first pronounce the Benediction, then you will get the pudding," the servant insisted.

"How does that concern you? I'll pronounce the Benediction without you. You give me the pudding."

"You are the wicked Esau himself, and you are liable, God forbid, to eat without a Benediction."

There was no help for it, and Shlomele had to comply with the servant's demand, although it gave him pain that the Christian woman was looking out for his religious observances. But, as the fragrance of the blackberry pudding which the servant held reached his nostrils and made his mouth water, he pronounced the Benediction and was given the pudding. Over the pudding friendly relations between husband and wife were re-established. Soon they were sitting together in perfect domestic tran-

quillity on the doorstep of the inn, and sharing the
pudding between them.

But they were not allowed to sit long together in
peace. Mendel's voice made itself heard from the
inn.

"Shlomele! Shlomele!"

And Marusha appeared in the doorway. "Go
into the house, young rascal, your father wants you
to go and open the church for the peasants."

When Shlomele came into the inn, he found his
father in the center of a circle of Russian peasants
and peasant women, and one peasant, half naked,
barefooted and bareheaded, wearing only a long
shirt, was holding in his arms an infant wrapped in
rags and kneeling before Mendel.

"Dear little father, have pity, let us have the key
for the church, so we can christen the child. It is
already four months old and not yet sprinkled with
God's water. He may die unchristened, and then
the devil will take him away."

"Yes, and then some of you will tell the Polish
priest that I gave the key without the fee, and he
will have me flogged as he did at the time of Yephrem's
wedding. The Jew gets plenty of lashes for his own
religion, and I have no desire to be flogged for another.
I'll not do it."

"May we be stricken dumb, may our mouths be
paralyzed if we say a single word," the half naked
peasant besought Mendel, kneeling in front of him.
"Help, dear little father. The child is sick and is
liable to die. It will fall into the hands of the devil,

and then come and choke its father. Have pity, dear little father."

"Take the key, Shlomo, and open the church for the peasants," and Mendel gave Shlomele the key, which hung on the nail together with the keys of the rooms where he stored the brandy.

"God will repay you, dear little father, God will repay you," and the half naked peasant kissed Mendel's boots and followed Shlomo with the infant in his arms.

"Come, Father, do God's work, the Jew has granted the key." The peasant turned to the Greek Orthodox Priest who was sitting on the bench near the oven.

But the priest did not stir. With his broad back he hid the oven from view and remained sitting as though he were plastered to the wall.

"What are you waiting for, Little Father?" Mendel asked him.

"There was a thimbleful of holy spirits in the church and the souls drank it, and without holy spirits God will not receive the soul into the Christian faith," the priest replied.

"What do you want?"

"Do a Christian deed, Mendel, help a poor naked soul to come into the Christian faith by contributing a bottle of wine for the church," and the priest pulled an empty flask from his broad pocket and held it towards Mendel. "God will pay you for it. We are poor folk."

"Woe is me, he is beginning again! What does

this lumbering creature want of me? The Polish priest will flog me to death. Haven't I a wife and a child? I am not helping, I am not doing anything, I know of nothing whatever. You want the key to the church,—here take it. I have no need for it for myself. You want brandy,—here take some brandy. That's what I keep the inn for,—to sell brandy. But how am I helping you? How, I ask? I am not helping at all. I am doing nothing at all. I know of nothing," and Mendel poured a measure of brandy into the flask for the priest, and pushed him out of the inn.

Shlomele opened the church for the priest and ran away swiftly so as not to touch the walls of the church. He stopped at a distance so as not to become "unclean" from hearing the singing in the church. And when the priest's bass voice reached him none the less, he covered his ears with his hands in order not to hear the sounds, which would stupefy his mind against the study of the Torah.

His father waited for him near the door of the inn with a bundle of clean linen under his arm, and took him to the communal bath for the Sabbath ablutions, for the sexton had proclaimed in the market-place of the town that the bath was ready.

On getting home from the bath, all clean and dressed in clean shirts with broad white collars folded over their long green coats, they found the inn transformed into a peaceful Sabbath nest. There was nothing in evidence which could remind one of an inn. The kegs of brandy were covered with white sheets, and

before the shelves were hung shawls and curtains.
The inn was tidied up and transformed into a Sabbath
home looking as though no buying and selling of
any sort had ever been conducted there. Seven
pure tallow candles burned in the large brass candlestick, on the base of which sparkled the words in
Hebrew: "Lights for the Sabbath." Two pairs
of white loaves, one large pair for the master of
the house and one small one for the young husband,
were set upon the white linen-covered table together
with a large silver cup and a small silver cup. And
the mother with her daughter-in-law sat by the table,
both dressed in long trailing coats of green silk and
new lace head-dresses. Their white foreheads were
bound with fillets, and on their bosoms sparkled the
plates studded with jewels which they had received
from their husbands. Little Deborah, looking as
though she were disguised as a young wife, aped
everything that her mother-in-law did, and Marusha,
dressed for the Sabbath in a new apron and a new
headkerchief, sat on a little stool near the oven and
gazed with pride on the young mistress. Mother
and daughter sang together a song in honor of the
Sabbath before the blessing of the candles:

A pleasant song I now will sing,
With joyful voice which loud shall ring,
In honor of the holy Queen far-famed:
Sabbath is the name by which she is named.

God, with whom doth ever dwell the light,
May He send unto my home the Sabbath bright;

For her dear sake my house I purified,
Why lingers she so long outside?

Six long days she roams in sun and rain
Like one who doth in exile suffer bitter pain;
Even like a bird from roof to roof she flies
Until the hour when holy Sabbath hither hies.

And when Shlomele had taken the large prayer
book and was ready to go with his father to the
synagogue, there was heard the noise of a big Polish
equipage with many horses, which stopped in front
of the inn.

"Hey there, Jew, open! His Exalted Excellency,
Pan Dombrowski, is knocking at your door.   Open!"

"Heavens, his great Excellency Pan Dombrowski
is knocking at my door! I cannot, I cannot, dear
master, it is the Sabbath now."

"Jew, I will have thirty lashes given you. Open
the door!"

"I must not, dear master.   It is the Jew's Sabbath
now!"

"How dare you, Jew? His Exalted Excellency,
Pan Dombrowski, desires a glass of whiskey."

"I cannot, dear master, I must not, dear master,
it is the Sabbath now."

"Put a measure of brandy down behind the door.
Not a drop to be had in the whole city."

"I cannot, dear master, my wife has already lighted
the candles."

"Accursed Jew! When the Jew keeps his Sabbath
all Poland must be without brandy," said a voice
from the other side of the door.

CHAPTER SIX

To the Yeshivah

When Shlomele was fourteen years old, they made ready to send him to the famous Yeshivah of Lublin, where all Jewish young men of good family went to study. Mendel was planning to go to Lublin for the annual fair where the Assembly of the Four Countries, the Jewish Parliament, was to convene that year. Mendel desired to present himself to this body for the first time as *parnas*, and, also, to submit for its consideration an important matter which concerned the general Jewish welfare.

One fine Friday afternoon the little tailor, Shlomele's teacher, appeared in Zlochov. As soon as the Sabbath was over, he sat down behind the oven in Mendel's inn, armed with needle and thimble, to sew garments for Shlomele to take along on his journey. The little tailor made garments on the same principle as did the Jews of old in the desert, so that the garments might grow along with the wearer. The lower edge he folded under so that by taking out the seam the garment could be made longer. Out of one of Mendel's old garments the little tailor made a wadded winter overcoat for Shlomele. He made him a fancy coat of purple silk for Sabbaths and holidays, a pair of broad trousers of black calico and several coarse linen shirts. The little tailor sewed

the garments in accordance with all the religious
prescriptions, with round corners so as to exempt them
from the necessity of having fringes, guarding care-
fully against a mixture of wool and silk, not wasting
a moment during his work and singing Psalms or
studying the Mishnah, which he knew by heart.

It was rumored concerning the little tailor that
he was a *Tzaddik* incognito, one of the "thirty-six"
by whose grace the world exists. The little tailor
used to disappear from the town for several weeks
at a time and to live in the deep forests. Sometimes he would put in a sudden appearance, the day
before the Sabbath, at the home of a solitary Jewish
innkeeper and pronounce the *Kiddush* for the un-
lettered man; or he would appear before a lonely
woman in labor in the dead of night in some out-of-
the-way inn, and wage war against the Lilith who
had come to slay the child. Rumor had it that unto
the little tailor in the forest used to come the souls of
great scholars, who taught him the mysteries of
the Torah. The garments which the little tailor
sewed were a charm against various diseases. They
would clothe in them a person who was dangerously
ill, and he became well, or a woman in hard labor
with child, and the child was born.

In Mendel's home the little tailor was regarded
as a holy person, and his sewing as holy work. Silence
reigned near the large oven where the little tailor
sat and sewed garments for Shlomele. They were
sure that the little tailor's garments would protect
him from all evil, and guard him throughout the

long period when Shlomele would be far from home among strangers.

On the Sabbath before Shlomele left for the Yeshivah, he was sitting in the large room on the wooden bench studying his portion of the Talmud. No one else was in the room, his parents being asleep. Whereupon the old servant Marusha took little Deborah, his wife, and decked her out in her finest clothes. A white, embroidered bonnet came down over her ears, and she wore a white embroidered apron over her green silk dress. Marusha gave her a pear and an apple and sent her in to Shlomele. The old woman herself stood behind the door and looked in through a crack. Seeing her husband, Deborah remained standing near the door, stuck her finger into her mouth and with the other hand held her white apron. Shlomele continued his Talmudic chant, throwing now and then a glance in her direction. All at once his little wife approached him and remained standing near him. Shlomele closed the large Talmud folio and looked at her.

For a long time husband and wife looked at each other in silence. Then the little girl took into her hand one of the fringes of his long four-fringed garment, which almost covered him completely.

"You are going away?"

"Yes," Shlomele nodded.

"I don't want you to go away."

"I must go to the Yeshivah to study the Torah,— the rabbi has ordered it."

"And when will you come back?"

"When I shall be all grown up, and a first class student of Holy Torah."

Again the child was silent for a few moments. Then she suddenly exclaimed:

"I want to go home to my mother."

"You cannot go home to your mother. You must stay here, because you are wedded to me in accordance with the law of Moses and Israel."

"I am not wedded to you."

"Do you remember when we both stood under the canopy the day when the synagogue was dedicated and I placed a little ring on your finger?"

The little girl could find no answer to this.

"But I want to go home. I don't want to stay here," the little girl exclaimed, suddenly bowing her head towards him.

"Why?"

"Just so."

"Why, just so?"

"Because you are going away."

"And if I will bring you something when I come back, will you stay here?"

"What will you bring me?"

"What should I bring you?"

"A pair of golden slippers like your mother's, with high heels."

"Very well, I'll bring them for you."

"With golden laces?"

"Yes. And you will not go home?"

"No, I will not even cry."

"If so, then I like you," Shlomele answered, stroking her head-dress.

"And I like you, too," said Deborah, pulling at the fringe of his garment.

Husband and wife were again silent a while. Suddenly Deborah remembered something.

"Will you have an apple?"

"Yes," the boy nodded.

Deborah took the apple out of the pocket of her apron and gave it to him.

"Where did you get it?"

"Marusha gave it to me. An apple for you and a pear for me." And the girl took the pear out of the other pocket.

The two sat down on the bench to eat the fruit.

"Here, taste my pear," says the little wife.

"Taste my apple," says the little husband.

————

The following morning, when the first rays of the red sun, which lighted up half the heavens, had removed the shroud of night from the earth, Hillel the driver stopped his hooded van in front of the inn. From the inn they began to carry out pillows and covers and shawls, and big and little bags of food and kegs of brandy, provisions for the journey from Zlochov to Lublin, which would take two to three weeks. Chayim the Postman, or, as he was called, "the Guardian of Israel," also got into the van. He was taken along as a defense against brigands.

Chayim was a tall, powerful Jew who was able to ride a horse and, alone of all the Jews of the town,

knew how to use gun and powder. He was dressed
in his official uniform of a Jewish policeman, with
one gun in front and another behind, and around his
waist a big belt, from which hung down his powder
horn.

Chayim was a public personage. He was officially
employed as court messenger and he was especially
useful when there was need of sending a messenger
from one settlement to another on an important
mission, or when the officials had to hail before the
court a defiant person who refused to come, in which
case Chayim the Postman was sent to bring him by
force. Chayim the Postman was charged with all
the duties in the town which required the use of
force, and since his person alone was not endowed
with too much strength he provided himself with
arms.

Another passenger in the van was Reb Jonah
Eibeschutz, the lay-preacher of the town, who preached
a sermon every Sabbath afternoon, in which he pic-
tured in vivid colors Hell and all its burning pits,
as well as Heaven and all its circles. Reb Jonah was
as well posted on Hell, as familiar with all its lime-
kilns and boiling cauldrons, as if he were a resident
there. He had collected all his sermons into a book,
which he was taking to Lublin to lay before the
Assembly of the Four Countries and get permission
to publish it. At the same time, also, he expected
to obtain an endorsement of his book from one of
the celebrities, and in addition, at the fair, where so
many wealthy merchants were assembled, to look

around for a rich man who might wish to earn for himself a portion of the World-to-Come by assuming the expenses of publication.

At length there came out of the inn Mendel and his son Shlomele. Old Marusha, who carried his little trunk, expressed the wish in Yiddish that his thirst for learning should be very great. His mother and little wife stood before the door of the inn.

"Why don't you say good-bye to your wife, Shlomele? A husband who goes away for such a long time should say farewell to his wife," said his father.

Shlomele, dressed in the long coat which trailed at his feet and a big yellow fur hat, approached Deborah who stood near her mother-in-law, and with averted eyes said:

"Good-bye, Deborah."

The girl was silent.

"Say to your husband: 'A pleasant journey to you, and may you be eager for learning,'" her mother-in-law coached her.

"A pleasant journey, and may you be eager for learning," the girl repeated. And for the first time since their marriage the two children were ashamed to look one another directly in the face.

Shlomele was ready to get into the van, but at the last moment the mother was unable to restrain herself. She seized her only son and covered him with tears and kisses.

"May God be your protector when I am not near you!" And after her came the Cossack servant.

Only the little wife looked down earnestly at the ground.

"Yocheved," Mendel reminded his wife, "God has privileged you to send your son to the Yeshivah, where there are great scholars and Geonim, and you are weeping."

"For God's great kindness," said the mother, wiping her tears with her apron.

Shlomele brushed his mother's kisses from his cheek with his sleeve and jumped into the van.

"With the right foot first, on the right road,
Where lurks no evil spirit
But only the good,
And nothing but peace..."

was the wish his mother spoke after him.

―――――

Slowly the wagon passed through the drowsy little town, and came out among the fields of the big estates of the nobles. The sheaves of grain in the fields were golden in the sunlight. The grass was wet with the dew of the morning, and in the fresh and transparent air little clouds of smoke mounted from the straw-thatched roofs of the peasants and imparted a homelike aspect to the entire landscape. But the farther they travelled and the higher the hot sun rose as the day advanced, the more scarce became the cultivated fields, and the earth spread out in every direction in endless expanse.

And Mendel's van seemed lost in an uncharted sea of tall, fragrant weeds studded with many-colored flowers. As far as eye could reach nothing could be

seen but God's green world. Here and there a clump
of young white willows stood out on a little hill,
weaving a delicate tracery with their long tender
branches, and behind the tracery stray white cloudlets were visible, moving like flocks of sheep across
the limitless sky.

Here and there the little trees threw their shadows
over the field, and the shadowed green portion stood
out in strong contrast on the sun-smitten field.
And elsewhere a clump of wild, red poppy heads
blazed in the light of the sun. Thus did the steppe
flaunt the light and colors of its many-hued flowers
and weeds for no one but itself alone and God, its
Creator.

The narrow path which led uphill from the city
and then into the valley was lost in the sea of green.
They were unable to make out whither the road led.
Then Hillel the driver gave his horses free rein to
enable them to scent out the river Uman. The horses
raised their heads several times, distended their
moist nostrils and sniffed the air loudly. Then their
necks sank deeper into their collars and with greater
speed they moved forward into the heart of the steppe.

CHAPTER SEVEN

In the Heart of the Steppe

A mysterious fear seized upon the hearts of our travellers when the vehicle entered into the depths of the steppe. They cast uneasy glances around them, looking to see if a green Tatar cap would not suddenly make its appearance among the grass or if the white sheepskin cap of a Cossack would not peep out from the bushes. The steppe, as far as Uman, was not safe. Swimming across the Dnieper, Zaporozhian Cossacks would come from the other side, and lie in wait for Jewish merchants. Even the Tatars in their light boats would come down the Dniester from their country and hide in the grass of the steppe, lying in wait for the Jewish travellers whom they would capture and take to the slave markets of Constantinople or Smyrna, where they knew that the Turkish Jews would pay large ransoms for them. Mendel's heart was filled with apprehension, and he looked hopefully and trustingly at his defender, Chayim the Postman, who was sitting on the box of the wagon. But the "Guardian of Israel" sat curled up in the box, his nose buried in the forest of hair of his mustaches, his eyes closed under their beetling black brows, sleeping the sleep of the just.

But Mendel and his fellow-travellers were afraid of the steppe without reason. Nothing was so peace-

ful as the steppe, nothing so peaceful as the play of
colors of its millions of weeds and flowers, nothing so
peaceful as the song of a million notes which it sang
in the glorious sunlight. The numerous varieties
of bees and other insects buzzed and swarmed among
the weeds, looking like a transparent, multi-colored
cloud of dust above the flowers. Living, winged
blossoms rose into the air,—the many-colored butterflies, which emerged from the flowers and glowed with
the same tints and hues. The day shone full upon the
steppe, and the sun warmed every blade of grass.
The steppe was redolent with fragrance. The sweet
smell of honey was distilled from the white flowers
and imbued every creature with sweet, drowsy desire and longing. At times the tramping of the horses'
feet awakened a sleeping flock of birds. From the
midst of the tall grasses swarms of blackbirds rose
up into the air and circled above the vehicle, waking
every sleeping creature in the weeds with their cries
and with the whirring of their wings. Then was the
whole steppe awake. It became alive with the language
of winged and creeping things, of things that
blossomed and sprouted. From every bush and tuft
of flowers variegated clouds of butterflies rose up,
awakened by the cries of the birds. And now
there was no telling which were the flowers and
which the insects.

Sometimes the wagon came upon a hidden brook.
They were surprised to see a little spring emerge
suddenly from among the weeds and over it a solitary bird of prey in wait for some fish or insect which

circled about on the rippled surface. The lonely
bird of prey was frightened by the hoofs of the horses
and rose up into the clouds, waking the steppe with
his screams of alarm. He was answered by invisible
creatures who were hidden somewhere in the depths
of the weeds, and they seemed to be relaying the bad
tidings one to another: Run, run! Man has come
to conquer the steppe!

But our travellers perceived nothing of all this.
They were occupied each with his own affairs.
Hillel the driver became a bit drowsy after having
eaten too well of the stuffed tripe which Yocheved
had given him for the journey and which had remained
over from the feast held in honor of the departing
Sabbath. The scent of honey penetrated the very
marrow. The mouth became dry and the odors of
the steppe rose to the head and made one drowsy.
And so, after the horses were no longer in need of
their guide, Hillel fell asleep. Nevertheless the horses
were aware of the waking nose of their master instead of his sleeping eye.

His snoring infected the "Guardian of Israel",
Chayim the Postman. Just as Hillel was a great
glutton, so was Chayim a hard drinker. "He was
in no wise able to display his strength, of which the
community stood in such great need, except he did
first enkindle his anger by means of brandy." (This
is officially recorded concerning him in the Chronicle
of Zlochov.) Being a prudent Jew with a wife
and several children, he could not otherwise "risk
his life" and take up the "destroyer", his gun, un-

less he had first taken several drinks. When sober, he was afraid of a gun, of a horse and of a dog like every other Jew, and when it was necessary to send him on a mission across the steppe to the next town, or to have him hail a refractory personage to the bar of justice, or to have him punish someone with flogging or chain someone in the little prison, he was unable to discharge these duties unless he first filled himself with drink. Before Mendel undertook the journey to Lublin across the steppe, he first gave him a good many draughts, and during the entire trip Chayim maintained his warlike spirit and heroic courage with the fiery stuff which inspired him with the daring of a Polish Lord. And now, also, sitting on the box, he flaunted his courage by keeping his gun on his shoulder for no particular reason at all, which inspired Mendel with a great fear lest the "destroyer" go off of itself. But when Chayim perceived that there was as yet no need of his courage, since no brigands were to be seen, and that the warlike mood which the spirits had aroused was going to waste, he gave vent to his ferocity in his snoring. The sounds issuing from his broad nostrils, which gaped from his hairy face like two chimneys out of a straw roof, were like the rattling of a cracked hunting-horn.

The driver and the guard continued to sway on the box of the wagon until they fell into one another's arms in an affectionate embrace. Their snoring united into a discord which scared the hares out of their hiding places.

Mendel and Reb Jonah, however, talked enough to make up for those who slept. After conquering his fear of the Cossacks, Mendel began to look around him and observe God's world, and seeing how immense and devoid of human beings it was, he conceived the desire of planting Jewish settlements over the entire steppe. What numbers of Jewish cities and towns could be built on the steppe, and synagogues, schools, ritual-baths and Yeshivahs! And trade also: every month a different fair in a different city. The fields are covered with crops, and busy roads lead from one city to the other, and Jews traverse the roads with loads of merchandise and engage in trade. And the Torah is diffused over all of Ukraine, for where there is bread there also is Torah. And Mendel, himself, is a great merchant, and a parnas over an entire settlement...He communicated his thoughts to Reb Jonah.

"Very big is God's world, Reb Jonah," said Mendel with a sigh. "And the soil over which we are passing is good soil, Reb Jonah, black soil. You can tell it by the weeds. Where we are passing, Reb Jonah, there will some day be Jewish settlements. Jewish towns will lie scattered over the whole land. Jews will trade, will carry merchandise from one city to another, will build Yeshivahs, and the Torah will be spread broadcast."

For a minute Reb Jonah was silent, pondering on what Mendel had said. Then he replied:

"The soil here is good soil, the land is broad, but there is no one here to remember God's Name, to

pronounce a Benediction, to say prayers, therefore
it is filled with demons and evil spirits. And do
you think, parnas, that those are ordinary birds which
follow our wagon, ordinary weeds or bees and insects?
Those are all souls, lost and roaming in the forests
and deserts, awaiting redemption. Seeing a wagon
with Jews, they follow us, trying to catch a word of
the Torah or a Benediction, so that they might
through us obtain redemption and have peace...
If it will please God that Jews come and settle here,
build synagogues and schools, pray and praise the
Lord, they will drive away the evil spirits. It will
become a clean place and a human settlement."

"Do you think, Reb Jonah, that there will ever be
a settlement here with Jewish towns and synagogues?"

"Of course! How then? The place is specially
intended for Jews. When the Gentiles had greatly
oppressed the exiled Jews, and the Divine Presence
saw that there was no limit and no end to the oppres-
sion and that the handful of Jews might, God forbid, go under, the Presence came before the Lord
of the Universe to lay the grievance before Him, and
said to Him as follows: 'How long is this going to
last? When You sent the dove out of the ark at the
time of the flood, You gave it an olive branch so
that it might have a support for its feet on the water,
and yet it was unable to bear the water of the flood
and returned to the ark; whereas my children You have
sent out of the ark into a flood, and have provided
nothing for a support where they may rest their
feet in their exile.' Thereupon God took a piece

of Eretz Yisroel, which he had hidden away in the heavens at the time when the Temple was destroyed, and sent it down upon the earth and said: 'Be My resting place for My children in their exile.' That is why it is called Poland (Polen), from the Hebrew *poh lin*, which means: 'Here shalt thou lodge' in the exile. That is why Satan has no power over us here, and the Torah is spread broadcast over the whole country. There are synagogues and schools and Yeshivahs, God be thanked."

"And what will happen in the great future when the Messiah will come? What are we going to do with the synagogues and the settlements which we shall have built up in Poland?" asked Mendel as he suddenly thought of Zlochov.

"How can you ask? In the great future, when the Messiah will come, God will certainly transport Poland with all its settlements, synagogues and Yeshivahs to Eretz Yisroel. How else could it be?"

Mendel was completely satisfied, not only with regard to his own Zlochov, but the whole of Poland, whose destiny, after the coming of the Messiah, he could never get clear in his mind.

And after Mendel had satisfied the hunger of his spirit, his bodily hunger began to assert itself. Hillel the driver with his wistful glances helped to remind him of it, and the "Guardian of Israel" scratched his head, his beard and his ear-locks all the time that the lay-preacher was speaking. The air of the steppe, moreover, stimulated the appetite.

And soon they found a brook, where they stopped and washed their hands.

Yocheved's large, dried cakes of cheese, black radishes and strong spirits strengthened the body as did the words of Reb Jonah the soul. And when body and soul were satisfied, they all surrendered to the power of sleep and left it to the horses to find their own way to Uman. And the horses scented the forest of Uman from the steppe, and when the sun began to set and united sky and steppe in one fiery red flame, the forest of Uman appeared like a black band on the horizon, and, together with the quiet evening, they passed through the gate of Uman.

CHAPTER EIGHT

THE CONFERENCE OF PARNASIM

Several days later, Mendel's wagon stopped before the inn of Boruch Shenker on the Jewish street of Nemirov. Hillel found the entrance to the inn blocked with covered vans and vehicles of all sorts.

"Ho there! Make room for the parnas of Zlochov! Move up there, you scab-head, the plagues of Egypt on your head! Make room, make room, make room, the parnas of Zlochov is coming! Did you hear?" the driver shouted.

"Don't shout so, servant of King Rags! The plagues of Egypt and the curses of anathema in addition be laid out on your head. Reb Zechariah Sobilenky, the parnas of Chihirin,—it is his van that is standing here. Show respect!" they cried from the other van.

On hearing whose van it was, Mendel ordered the driver to stop, alighted from his van and approached the other.

"Is Reb Zechariah here?"

"Yes. He came with his brother Reb Jacob, and they are going to Lublin to the fair. They have stopped at the house of the head of the Yeshivah, Reb Yechiel Michel, and ordered us to stand here with the van over night."

Reb Zechariah, the parnas of Chihirin, rode with

two braces of horses like the great lords, and his van
was very big and crammed with pillows and covers.
It blocked the whole entrance. Mendel ordered his
driver to pull up to one side, and take the horses
to the stable and feed them well. He then went
into the hotel, and the driver and guard soon followed him with his parcels and pillows. Mendel
put on his new coat, dressed his son Shlomele in his
best clothes and went down to present himself to the
head of the Yeshivah, Reb Yechiel Michel the rabbi
of Nemirov.

In the audience room of Reb Yechiel Michel he
found the parnasim of Uman and Karsoon, the two
brothers, Reb Zechariah and Reb Jacob Sobilenky
of Chihirin, as well as the parnasim and prominent
residents of the city of Nemirov, who came to greet
the out-of-town parnasim. Reb Yechiel Michel was
not there. He was still in the yeshivah, where he
was expounding the portion of the Talmud before
the students. And the attendants in the meantime
placed before the parnasim, on behalf of the rabbi's
mother, honey cakes and red brandy.

Reb Zechariah Sobilenky, the parnas of Chihirin,
sat with an air of importance on the wooden bench.
The Sobilenkys looked upon themselves as very
important personages, and this was especially true
of Reb Zechariah, who was held in high regard by
the magnate Konitz-Polski, the lord of Chihirin,
who was also lord of Zlochov, so that Mendel, too,
was under his jurisdiction. Mendel had great respect for Zechariah as an older parnas. Mendel knew

that he would not find it easy to be accepted among the parnasim, and he was a little afraid. He looked with deference at Reb Zechariah who sat with his broad and long yellow beard spread out on his chest, his eyes hidden under his beetling yellow brows, and his sun-tanned face covered with freckles which looked like islands in a large yellow sea. Reb Zechariah paid no attention to him. He did not even notice the new parnas of Zlochov.

"Peace unto you, parnas of Zlochov", was the greeting which Mendel received from Reb Sholom Jacob, the chief parnas of Nemirov.

"Unto you peace," was Mendel's answer.

"What news from Zlochov? It is said that Zlochov is growing into a populous city in Israel. It will soon be as large as Chihirin," said the parnas of Nemirov with the intention of piquing the great Zechariah.

"With the help of God, our settlement keeps on growing."

Zechariah lifted his thick yellow eyebrows and looked around. He understood the innuendo which Sholom Jacob the parnas of Nemirov intended for him in comparing the village of Zlochov to the community of Chihirin, which was a large and populous settlement. But it was not easy to ruffle the equanimity of Reb Zechariah. He lifted his eyebrows only once, and lowered them again.

Between the magnate of Chihirin, Lord Konitz-Polski, and the magnate of Nemirov, Prince Vish-newetzki, there was continuous rivalry for the suzerainty of Ukrainia.   Lord Konitz-Polski had possession of the entire steppe which bordered on the "Yellow River" as far as the *Setch*.   Vishnewetzki, however, bore the title of Prince of "Russ".   This rivalry was not without its effect on the Jews of the two magnates, but it affected especially the parnasim of the two cities, who were the intermediaries for the Jews with their respective lords.   The parnasim were so deeply involved in the rivalry of their masters that it virtually became their own.   They vaunted the wealth and possessions of their respective lords, and whenever the two parnasim met, the contest flared up.

"What, after all, does Chihirin amount to?   It is a large community of Cossack peasants.   With the help of God Zlochov will surpass it."   Reb Sholom Jacob gave Zechariah another dig.

But this time Zechariah could not brook it.   He, who is held in such high esteem by his lord who consults him in all his affairs, to be compared with this Mendel of Zlochov!   He lifted his eyebrows again and turned to Mendel:

"Are you the Mendel of Zlochov who got permission to build a synagogue?   My Lord told me about it.   *Sholom Aleichem*," and Zechariah extended his hand from a distance without rising from his place of honor on the wooden bench.   "And who is the young man?"   Zechariah asked, pointing to Shlomele.

"This is my son, married, with God's help, and going to Lublin to the Yeshivah."

"To Lublin? Are there not enough yeshivahs here in Podolya, in Kremenetz, in Lvov? And right here in our own section there is Reb Yechiel Michel's. What? Has this young man of yours become so great a scholar in Zlochov that you have not been able to find a yeshivah for him in the whole of Podolya, but you must take him all the way to Lublin?"

"The Rabbi, his father-in-law, has given him letters to the great Reb Naphtali Katz, the rabbi of Lublin. The boy has a good head," Mendel explained. "And, at the same time, we want him to learn secular subjects also, to be able to figure well and to talk with the officials, because Zlochov is growing, with God's help, and we shall need a Jewish representative who is able to speak Polish."

These words annoyed Zechariah even more. He replied with heat:

"He could learn Polish from the peasants in Zlochov."

Mendel remained silent out of respect for an old parnas. But that was too much for Reb Sholom Jacob.

"What! Does the parnas of Chihirin think that he alone obtained permission from the Assembly to be a Jewish representative? You are doing well, Reb Mendel, in sending your young man to Lublin," Reb Sholom Jacob reassured Mendel. "We need to have in our parts honest parnasim, such as work in communal affairs with sincerity of heart, not like certain ones who remove the pearls from the Ark-curtains and stud them into honey cakes as gifts for magnates in order to find favor in their eyes."

"My brother did not take the pearls for himself, God forbid!" Reb Jacob Sobilenky defended his brother. "The parnas of Chihirin took the pearls from Jewish matrons of that city and made of them a precious gift for the Magnate Konitz-Polski, may his glory be exalted, by whose grace we all live in peace and security, on the occasion of his marriage with the rich Countess Zamoyski."

"Naturally, when a pauper married a Zamoyski he must have recourse to the Jews of his cities for his wedding expenses. Who is he anyway? A Vishnewetzki? The Vishnewetzkis don't need to depend on Jewish pearls when they get married."

An offense against himself Reb Zechariah was able to ignore, but the insult against his lord he could not tolerate.

"Parnas of Nemirov, you are playing with fire. You are insulting my noble lord."

"And if so, what of it? I am not afraid of your lord. Will you have me put into prison perhaps as you did Captain Chmelnitzki? We are living here, God be praised, under Prince Vishnewetzki who is a merciful ruler, so I have no fear whatever of your master, parnas of Chihirin."

Who knows how this quarrel would have ended if the attendant had not suddenly opened the door and announced: "Reb Yechiel Michel is on his way!"

All rose from their places and Reb Yechiel Michel entered. The rabbi was still a young man, but he

was already famed throughout Podolya and Volhynia
as the Gaon of Ukrainia. He enjoyed the respect
of all men. The rabbi first stepped into another room
and conducted thence his old mother, whom he seated
in the place of honor in an armchair near the table.
He then sat down on a smaller chair near her and in-
troduced to her the parnasim and notables, and
all the time waited on his mother with the greatest
deference and respect.

The rabbi questioned the parnasim on conditions
in their respective regions, how the settlements were
growing, and how matters stood with the study of
the Torah. On hearing that Mendel was taking his
son to the Yeshivah in Lublin he rejoiced greatly
that Zlochov was already privileged to send a student
to that great yeshivah. He put some questions
to Shlomele on his studies, which Shlomele answered
promptly to the great satisfaction of the rabbi, who
ordered the attendant to give him some honey cakes;
and Mendel wiped from his eyes the tears of joy.

"Your reverend teacher writes me to send him some
young men from my yeshivah to Zlochov to instruct
the children. The people of the town will give them
food and lodgings. Praised be the Lord of the Universe, the study of the Torah increases wherever
Jews live, even in the wild steppe," he said, turning
to his mother.

The old woman inclined her high festive headdress
of white lace which she had put on in honor of the
parnasim, and she whispered to her son:

"My son, offer the parnasim some brandy and cakes, to do them honor."

The rabbi rose to carry out his mother's command, and poured some brandy for the parnasim.

"And on what terms do you live with your neighbors? Is there peace between you? Your life is so exposed, living as you do in the open plain."

"To the best of our ability we strive to live in peace. The Polish magnates are absent throughout the year, and our only neighbors are the Russians; and since they are neighbors, we strive to live in peace with them. Very often they do not pay the church tax which the Polish priests have imposed upon them. They look upon it as an insult to their dignity, and so we do not exact it from them, but, instead, we collect the tax from among ourselves and pay it for them. But the Polish priests, becoming aware of this, took us severely to task. They compel us to exact the tax, and therein lies a great danger for us. We are afraid lest the Russians, God forbid, do us some evil. And that is what I have come to say to the rabbi of Nemirov. It would be very advisable that the parnasim of Ukrainia, together with the rabbis, should obtain from the Council in Lublin assurance that the Great Assembly will take up the matter and have the church tax on the Russians abolished, or else that Jews should not be forced to collect it, for that is liable to bring, God forbid, a great misfortune upon us. We live right near the steppe, and we hear it said that the Russians will one day avenge themselves upon us."

The rabbi sighed and remained silent.

"I, too, wish to speak on this matter," said Reb Sholom Jacob, the parnas of Nemirov. "The parnas of Chihirin, Reb Zechariah Sobilenky, is sitting here. The parnas of Zlochov, Reb Mendel, is afraid to speak out because he, together with the parnas of Chihirin, is subject to Konitz-Polski. But we here, God be praised, are under Prince Vishnewetzki, who is a merciful ruler to all. We are not afraid. And I desire to say here in the presence of the rabbi of Nemirov that it has reached our ears that the parnas of Chihirin, Reb Zechariah, oppresses very grievously the Jews and also the Russians. He imposes upon them very heavy taxes for gifts for his master. He has lodged information before his lord against one of their captains by the name of Chmelnitzki, saying that the aforesaid captain is planning to rebel, with the result that the captain has been thrown into prison. And because of that, the Russians are greatly incensed against the Jews, and a misfortune may come of it for the Jewish community at large."

During all the time that Reb Sholom Jacob brought the accusation against him, Reb Zechariah sat before the rabbi, proud and silent. With two of his fingers he combed his long, yellow beard, and kept lifting his thick yellow eyebrows, which were like two open fans on the ridge of his forehead above his eyes. From time to time he cast a glance from beneath them upon his opponent, and maintained his silence.

"Rabbi of Nemirov," Reb Zechariah began, "I

am not, God forbid, taking the taxes for myself. We Jews live only by the grace of the magnates, who protect us in their mercy from all evils, and grant us the privilege of building synagogues and establishing settlements, and we live with our families in peace and tranquillity as in no other land. Wherefore, we must be loyal to the Polish lords who rule over us with great mercy, and to the great and mighty King Vladislav, may his glory be exalted, who has renewed the privileges which the former Polish kings had granted us, and added new ones. We must be submissive and serve them faithfully, because, but for them, we might be like the Russian peasants, may God shield us! And when they order us to collect taxes from the Cossack peasants for the churches, we must carry out their decrees, because the peasants belong to the Polish lords for all time. And who is this Chmelnitzki about whom the parnas of Nemirov has raised such an outcry? He comes into my inn, and I hear him whisper with the peasants about writing a letter to the Khan of the Tatars and ask him to come and help the peasants free themselves from the Polish lords. He thinks I hear nothing, and I sit behind the table and pretend not to hear, but with a piece of chalk I make note of all the things that he says. Of course, it is my duty to deliver the captain into the hands of the authorities. My lord, may his glory be exalted, gave me permission, in case I hear such seditious talk from the Captain Chmelnitzki, to have him flogged before the door of my inn."

Reb Yechiel Michel remained absorbed in deep thought, then he turned to his mother and, bowing before her, spoke as follows:

"With my mother's permission, I will answer the parnas of Chihirin as follows: It is true that we live by the grace of the Polish lords and King Vladislav, may his glory be exalted, who has renewed the privileges of the Polish kings, peace unto them. But we do not live by their power but by the power of the Lord of the Universe and of the Holy Torah. And it is not they who are shielding us, but the Lord of the Universe in His great mercy. Our holy books enjoin us to live in peace with our neighbors and, above all, with such neighbors as are tormented and persecuted by their oppressors and whose faith is being humiliated. Their faith is not idol-worship. They believe in the only living God, and it is an act of piety to assist them so that they may be able to serve God according to their ways. We Jews should feel and realize what it means to be persecuted for one's faith. Therefore, I am much pleased with the good advice of the parnas of Zlochov that the Great Assembly shall seek to do something in the matter, that the representatives shall secure the abolition of the church tax, and, if that cannot be obtained, then we Jews shall not have anything to do with it. Parnas of Zlochov, I will, please God, give you a letter on this subject to take to the rabbi of Lublin."

At this point the attendant was heard knocking on the panels of the door with a wooden hammer. Thereupon the rabbi said:

"My friends, it is time for afternoon prayers," and, turning to his mother, he said, "With your permission, mother, we will rise."

"Yechiel Michel, after prayers you will invite the parnasim to have supper with us," his mother said, and rose from her place. And the son, with great reverence, conducted her to the threshhold of the next room.

CHAPTER NINE

THE PREACHER OF POLNO

A holy peace and purity lay upon the hills around the city of Nemirov, as the Jewish vans laden with bedding and passengers rolled joyously over the yellow sandy road. The night damp still lay heavy on the fields and on the road which led to the River Bug, but by the time they reached the other bank, the clear blue sky was already suffused with the light of the bright, newly-risen sun, which drank the dew from the grass and from the leaves of the tall sassafras trees that flanked the road. The golden yellow fields had already been reaped and harvested, and here and there a drab-gray linen peasant shirt was to be seen, or the flaming colors of a kerchief on the head of a peasant woman at work in the early morning. Fat sheep, overgrown with black wool, rolled like black balls on the broad fields and grazed at the hard stubble of the grain. They stopped munching and looked naïvely after the passing vans with their blank-staring eyes and called after them their quavering, child-like "ba-aa". From time to time the travellers came upon a sorrowful beggar sitting alone on a stone by the roadside twanging on a small home-made "lyre" and mumbling some song. Soon the cloud of dust which the vans left behind them covered the beggar, but his song affected the Jewish

travellers, and over God's joyous world there rang
out melodies from the Jewish Liturgy:
  "Come my beloved, come my beloved,
  Come my beloved, to meet the Bride,
  To meet the Sabbath Bride."

Our travellers no longer rode alone. As was natural,
the first in the procession was the big van of Reb
Zechariah with its two braces of horses, and it raised
high clouds of dust in front and behind. Then came
the other vans. Men of learning from the different
towns sat in the vans. Some were going to the Assembly to obtain answers to questions of ritual, others
to get permission to publish books of which they were
the authors. Many of the scholars and men of
learning assembled in one van. They sat at ease
amid the pillows and sheets and engaged in scholarly
disputation. One would clutch the beard of another
or grasp the lapels of his coat, forcing him to listen
to his involved interpretation, whereupon his opponent would stubbornly close his eyes and stick to
the negative, refusing to yield one iota. And the
loud disputes over the Torah re-echoed from the
vans, waking the sleeping hares of the fields, who ran
panic-stricken from the noise of the disputants.

Through the long winters the Jews of Podolya
manufacture out of leather the uppers for boots as
well as the soles, and take them to the annual fair
in Lublin. The makers of sheepskin coats bring
wagon-loads of these garments. The makers of

fur caps bring their wares, the potters bring their
vessels.   Some of the vehicles are filled with household utensils, others with prayer-shawls, four-fringed
garments, and the fringes themselves. The products
of the entire year are taken to the autumn fair, when
the noble proprietors, having gathered peasants'
crops into their barns, go to the fair to buy supplies
for the winter. The Jewish merchants run from one
van to another, strike bargains, exchange money, buy
up bales of flax, sacks of wool, calf-skins and spirits
as on a stock exchange. And marriage brokers speed
from one van to another and arrange matches and
betrothals of brides and bridegrooms who have never
seen each other, and the parents shake hands and
stop in the inns to drink each other's health. And
the drivers attempt to get ahead of each other, and
snatches of prayers from the holiday and Sabbath
services are lost amid the cracking of whips and the
clouds of dust.

Prayer services were conducted in the fields near
the brooks, among the tall trees. For the first
time those bare fields heard the sanctifications, and
the birds flocked to pick up the crumbs which remained
after the meals.

For the night they stopped in Bar. There was a
large Jewish community in that city, it was a gathering station for travellers from Vinitza, from Staro-
grad, from Karsoon and other points. There they
found more Jews, more scholars and merchants.
And into Constantinov there already entered a
caravan of vehicles laden with colored pillows and

sheets in the midst of which sat Jews at great ease. On the way all the synagogue melodies had been sung, the whole Torah had been disputed over, and half the country bought and sold. The settlements were now more numerous, the land populated, the towns with Jews and the villages with peasants. On every road they come upon a Jewish innkeeper where a halt is made to water the horses and to pronounce a benediction. In front of the inns stand the Jewish innkeepers in their colored trousers and broad four-fringed garments, and invite the scholars into their homes. They are eager for the privilege of having a *minyan* for afternoon prayers beneath their roof, and to see the men of learning drink each other's health.

And the innkeeper's wife hauls from the cellar great pots of buttermilk and cream and fried onions. At the same time, the innkeeper's children are examined, and the housewife is solemnly warned to be careful to observe all the religious rites. And marriage brokers make inquiries concerning brides and dowries, and they all drink out of the same flask, eat together, and take seats on each other's pillows as if the entire Jewish people had become one big family.

But soon they reached the big forest of Vishnewetz. The vehicles keep closer to each other, and the guards take out their "destroyers", of which the people are afraid. Far out in the woods among the dry leaves there is a rustling sound, and the travellers hold their breath and ask each other: "Did you hear that?"

And Jews tell each other stories of demons and

spirits who dwell in the woods, and throw a great
dread upon the young lads who are travelling to the
yeshivahs.   And the forest becomes more and more
dense and dark and mysterious.   The ancient trees
murmur as though surprised and afraid of the Jewish
vans which have entered their midst and awakened
them from their mysterious, age-long slumber.   The
sleeping beasts of the forest are frightened by the hoofs
of the horses.   In the distance can be heard their
roaring and the sound of their heavy feet among
the dry leaves.   The Kabbalists among the travellers
listen intently to the steps in the forest and whisper
mysterious prayers.   Fathers hang charms around
the necks of their children and place prayer books
in their hands.   The Jews take hold of the sacred
fringes of their garments to rout the evil spirits that
hover around the vehicles.   And the vans break
through the virgin forest, filled with the odor of resin,
which exudes from the trees, and with the damp odor
of mushrooms.   Someone is felling trees in the forest,
someone is shouting and calling for help in the forest,
and the Kabbalists stop their ears so as not to hear
the evil spirits calling.   The old Jews sing Psalms
and the children fall asleep in the midst of their
terror.

They stopped in Polno for the Sabbath, anxious
to hear Reb Simeon Ostropolier preach.   For years
this preacher had warned of impending calamities.
He frightened his audience so with his sermons that the
Assembly issued an injunction ordering him not to
alarm the people.   The sermons of the Ostropolier

were famed throughout the world. On the Sabbath afternoon Mendel took Shlomele with him and went to the synagogue where Reb Simeon preached. The synagogue already overflowed with Jews from the entire neighborhood. Whoever travelled to the annual fair stopped for the Sabbath in Polno in order to hear Reb Simeon. The walls of the synagogue were damp with the warm breath of the dense multitude. And on the elevation before the holy Ark stands Reb Simeon, dressed in a long white robe with a long prayer shawl draped about his tall emaciated body, his two black eyes flashing out of his pale face. It is full of fatigue, this pallid face of his, framed in his black beard; and, all atremble, he stretches his bony hands out of the sleeves of his white robe and emits a flood of fiery language, as he pictures to the vast throng the flames of Hell.

He leads them through all the seven circles of Hell. He shows how the angels of destruction snatch the human being as soon as he closes his eyes in death and carry him off to waste deserts, hurl him into swamps among serpents and scorpions; and the next minute they lead the victim away and leave him to float in a sea of fire with other unfortunates. And now he pictures before the frightened multitude the boiling cauldrons which are placed over the fires of Hell. Limbs of human beings float about in the seething cauldrons. And now he restores his victim to life so as to be able to torture him anew, to pull the hair out of his head with iron tongs, to rake his skin with iron combs and draw out his nails with red

hot pincers. Then he brings his victim back into
the world in the shape of a horse who toils all his
life for one whom he had wronged in his former life,
or he has his victim transformed into a wailing dog
who prowls about in waste deserts unable to find a
human settlement. A panic seizes upon the people.
Hot beads of perspiration appear on their faces. From
the women's synagogue a stifled sobbing is heard.

And the white-robed preacher continues to stand
over the vast throng, his bony hands outstretched,
uttering fearful threats, pouring the flames of Hell
over the heads of the Jews. He finds no one blame-
less enough to be immune from the pangs of Hell.
He transforms them all into new shapes, bringing
them back to earth in the form of cattle and other
animals, which yearn for a final resting-place.

Now, however, he begins to prophesy concerning
a terrible day of reckoning which is about to come
upon the Jews. He cites one Bible verse after another which points to the time, the time of the wars
of Gog and Magog, which are about to break out.
In vivid colors he pictures a great war, a
merciless enemy falling upon the land like a swarm
of locusts and with fire and sword destroying everything in his path. There is nothing that is able to
restrain him, no prayer, no supplication, no tears.
He moves like a conflagration from city to city,
from province to province, and consumes everything
with his fiery tongue, even as the ox doth consume
the grass. No one knows what the preacher is re-
ferring to. A dread fear, as when a dark cloud

suddenly covers the sky, falls upon the Jews. A shudder passes through them when he pictures God's wrath. One thing alone can hold up the dreadful decree: "Penitence, Prayer and Good Deeds." But now he shuts the Gate of Mercy, locks its iron doors, and stations in front of the Gate of Mercy fiery swords and fiery beasts to drive off the prayers of Jews which are knocking at the Gate. It is too late now, the awful decree has been signed, and he vouchsafes not a single ray of hope. There is nothing but darkness, darkness and darkness...

CHAPTER TEN

THE ANNUAL LUBLIN FAIR

After a journey of two weeks Hillel, with the "Guardian of Israel" on the box, rode through the Cracow gate into the famous city of Lublin. The spires and towers of its churches and castles had beckoned to them from a distance. From far away, Mendel had pointed out to Shlomele the spire of the synagogue of the famous scholar Rama. The annual fair was already in full swing. With much difficulty the driver steered his way through the multitude of *Pans'* coaches which stood on every hand. Hillel turned to a side road and came to the Jewish streets where the fair was at its height. Here lay heaps of fur coats, there hung rows of boots from wooden bars. There were stands heaped high with woolen cloth. Polish kerchiefs, vividly colored, blazed in the sun-light on the heads of the Jewish women standing at the booths and selling the wares: hues of golden yellow on a field of ivory. And a Babel of shouts and languages was borne on the air: German master craftsmen from Nuremberg were selling vessels of silver and brass, and even Persians came down with their Oriental fabrics of many colors: colors of amber and colors of ivory; hues of molten copper and transparent azure as of the sky; the deep blue of the night and the whiteness of snow; and shy colors as of the

foam, and the chaste hues of pearls beside the deep
glow of red beads—all these were merged into one
burning sea of fabrics, robes and carpets.

The colors moved as at a ball of masqueraders.
The heads of the generals and chamberlains, of the
hussars and ensigns blazed with tufts of many-
colored feathers. Here and there the flash of a
precious stone flared down from the turban on a
Tatar's head nodding above the sea of heads and
beckoning from afar.

Mendel was frightened by the great multitudes,
and so was Shlomele, and even the "Guardian of
Israel", Chayim the Postman, was frightened . Only
Hillel the driver was not afraid. Huddled in the box,
he held the horses firmly, picking his way among the
stands, the people and the wagons. He paid no attention to anything, refused to be concerned with
anything. He was engrossed in the work of steering
the horses, for the road was indeed a difficult one.

No easy matter did Mendel find it to secure a
lodging. Lublin was filled with Jews. From every
corner of Poland Jews came to Lublin to sell or buy
at the fair. From the farthest regions came rabbis
and parnasim with ritual questions and law-suits
for the "Assembly of the Four Countries", one
kehillah suing another and bringing its claims before
the rabbis. Each rabbi came with his disciples.
Students of the kabbalah in long white coats came
with the rabbi of Posen, Reb Sheftel Hurwitz, who
was a great student of the kabbalah. Keen minds,
great scholars, accompanied the rabbi of Lvov,

later the author of the "Taz," who was a member of
the Assembly. There were foreign Jews; Jews from
Germany in large velvet hats; Jews from Prague in
broad, black, silken cloaks; Italian Jews, whom it was
difficult to recognize as Jews, dressed as they were in
short, colored cloaks, like the Italians, with swords at
the side. Many of them came to trade or to study
at the yeshivah. Famed far and wide were the
yeshivahs of Poland, even as formerly the yeshivahs
of Babylon, and from all over the world Jews sent
their sons to study in the Polish yeshivahs. There
came many young men from different lands and provinces to obtain from this or the other great rabbi
who might attend the Assembly, certificates of or-
dination for the rabbinate. Authors came with their
books, seeking endorsements from the rabbis, and still
others sought permission to practice ritual slaughtering
or some other communal function.

And all these people wandered about in the little
Synagogue street where the rabbi dwelt, where the
great yeshivah was located and where the Assembly
was in session. In that street the Jewish fair was in
progress. On every hand were stands of Hebrew
books. There the marriage brokers had their head-
quarters, and to them came fathers who were anxious
to secure learned scholars as sons-in-law and made
their choice from among the students of the yeshivah
according to the dowry which they were able to offer.
There, also, various kabbalah specialists, followers
of Baal Shem Tob, had their booths where they sold
amulets against evil spirits and demons, and inscrip-

tions to hang on the wall against Lilith.   Pious women
in booths of their own sold special books of prayers
for women, charms for women in labor, deer's-teeth,
roots for sucklings, little waxen hands and feet, and
remedies for the toothache and for exorcizing the
evil eye.   In other booths sat scribes writing bills-of-
sale for merchants, notes and receipts for loans.
Young men drew artistic designs in colors for betrothal
contracts, marriage contracts and *Megillahs.* This
was an exclusive monopoly held by the students of
the yeshivah, the money going into a common fund
owned by the students.   Goldsmiths sold precious
ritual vessels, hammered kiddush-cups, lime-boxes
and spice-rods, also Chanukkah-lamps which made
music of themselves.   The principal traffic, however,
was in books.   The printers of Lublin, who were
authorized to print books uncensored, were celebrated
throughout the world, and Jews from all over the
world came to Lublin to buy Jewish books.   On
long tables in the synagogues and book-stalls the
volumes were on display, especially the famous Lublin
edition of the Talmud.   The vendors of prayer-
shawls had their stands there, displaying their woolen
prayer-shawls and immense fringes.   The gold and
silver neck-bands of the prayer-shawls flashed on the
stands.   Further on, in the little street near the entrance to the bath-house, the Jewish physicians had
their booths where they let bad blood, wrote prescriptions and extracted teeth.   There, also, the
female attendants of the ritual bath sold secret recipes
to childless women for having children, as well as

"indications" for giving birth to male children and
"indications" for female children; also spices and
herbs for winning the heart of a husband...And
Jews from all over Poland who, all year round, lived
like exiles in their inns, laid in stocks of Judaism to
last them throughout the winter. And among the
merchants went about the pious women who had
taken upon themselves the sacred duty of supplying
the students of the yeshivah with lodgings and other
necessities. They carried large tin boxes sealed with
the official seal of the yeshivah and cried: "Lodgings
for the young men! Shirts, boots for the students of
the Torah!"

After Mendel had given his son into the yeshivah,
he presented himself before the Assembly to bring
before them the matter of the church-tax which the
Polish nobility forced the Jewish inn-keepers to collect
from the Cossack peasants. With the letter which
the rabbi of Nemirov had given him to the author of
the Taz, he was admitted before the Assembly, which
was in session in the big hall of the Lublin community
house. The presiding officer was Reb Naphtali
Katz of distinguished ancestry, a grandson of the
rabbi of Lublin, himself of proud descent, and, on his
mother's side, a grandson of the Gaon of Prague.
In the Assembly sat great rabbis from Posen, Lvov,
and Cracow, and Jewish official representatives and
parnasim like Reb Abraham, the parnas of the Lublin
community, and Reb Moses Muntaltis, who was
descended from the Spanish exiles and very highly
regarded in the royal court. Thirty famous rabbis

and parnasim sat around the table. Before them Mendel presented his petition that the official representatives obtain the abrogation of the decree compelling the Jewish inn-keepers to collect the Church tax from the Cossacks, as otherwise a terrible calamity might come upon the Jews. The Assembly listened to Mendel, and the rabbi of Lublin said the proposal was a wise one. But the Assembly had also invited Zechariah Sobilenky, because he was a parnas from the same region and an important representative.

Reb Zechariah said there was danger that the proposal would provoke the wrath of the priests and the Jesuits. They will say that the Jews dissuade the peasants from becoming Catholics, and a great calamity may befall the Jews in consequence. And as soon as the Assembly heard mention of the word priests, a great dread fell upon all the famous rabbis and parnasim. Reb Sheftel Hurwitz, the rabbi of Posen, began to groan. He remembered the blood accusation of two years before in his district of Lenchitz and the martyrs which the priests had tortured to death. His pallid face took on a dark hue, his eyes withdrew underneath his forehead, and he sighed:

"A time of trouble is drawing nigh for Jacob."

And the *parnasim* replied that from the secular government they could obtain everything, but they were afraid to do anything touching the priests and the Church, because a great public calamity might result.

Thus they disposed of Mendel with a sigh and a

groan and sent him away to seek help from the Al-
mighty.   And thereupon Mendel set out for home.

And when he was already seated in his van together
with Chayim the "Guardian of Israel", and Hillel
the driver, he saw among the booths and stalls
of the little Synagogue street the devout little tailor,
Shlomele's first teacher, standing on the threshhold
of a stall and crying for buyers.   And he descended
from his van and entered the stall in order to buy
something, but he saw that the stall was empty, it
had nothing but four blank walls, and he asked
the little tailor:

"What have you to sell here?   Are you not here in
an empty stall?"

And the little tailor answered:

"I sell: Penitence, Prayers and Good Deeds!"

PART II

CHAPTER ONE

"It Has Begun"

For six years Shlomele attended the yeshivah of Lublin, preparing himself for the position which he was to occupy in life, the position of parnas of a Jewish community. He studied with the head of the yeshivah, the rabbi of Lublin, and, together with other young men, he had his lodging in the inn of Mistress Sarah Jaffe, who owned a large book printing establishment in the city. On Sabbaths and holidays he ate at her board where he learned good manners and customs, for she was a woman of high standing and, moreover, of princely generosity.

From home his mother used to send him, with the merchants who travelled to the annual fair, cakes of dried cheese or a jar of honey, and his father a pair of new boots, a sheepskin coat for the winter and a letter with greeting from "your wife," which began to awaken strange emotions in his heart and bring a flush to his cheeks.

At the end of six years, when Shlomele had completed the rabbinical course, and Mistress Deborah had grown to young womanhood, the parents of the couple met together and decided that, whereas it is not a good thing for a husband and wife to be separated, Shlomele should be brought home from the yeshivah.

Mendel travelled to Lublin to attend the fair, and to take his son home. The father did not recognize him. During those years Shlomele had matured, looking like a young rabbi with fur hat and ear-locks, and his father began to stand a little in awe of him. Shlomele inquired after everybody, after his mother and even after the servant Marusha, but not after his wife.

"And why do you not inquire after your wife?" his father smiled.

Shlomele flushed crimson.

"She has grown into a young woman, and beautiful, beshrew the evil eye, you will not recognize her. She is living with her parents."

"Why not with mother?" asked Shlomele.

"She is afraid of you, afraid that when you come home you will pull at her head-dress as you used to do when you were a child."

Shlomele was silent. Mendel was sorry for having embarrassed him.

"It is the custom, prior to the holidays and before the husband comes home, for the wife to stay with her parents. When, with the help of God, you will come home, she will come to live with us."

Shlomele would have liked to change the subject, but his father said:

"Here is some money, and buy something to take home for your wife as a holiday gift."

Shlomo took the money from his father to buy something for his wife. He went out to the fair, and came upon a Jew standing and calling:

"Golden slippers from Warsaw, holiday gifts for virtuous wives!"

Shlomo remembered the golden slippers which he had promised his wife before he left for the yeshivah.

He paid the merchant for the slippers, and the Jew pronounced the following wish:

"God grant that the righteous one who will wear these slippers may be privileged to wear them in holiness and purity."

He gazed upon the Jew. The latter seemed familiar to him, as though he had seen him somewhere before.

Afterwards Shlomo remembered that the Jew was the little tailor, and the thing appeared to him strange.

———

It was in the year 5408 (C. E. 1647), just before the festival of Purim. Across the white fields a peasant's sleigh filled with passengers glided merrily. The shadows of the passengers, horses and sleigh crept across the field behind the equipage. The muddy road wound up hill and down valley in the broad white expanse. Here and there broad black fields already dotted the sea of white like islands. It was towards evening after a fine sunny day. The sky overhead was bright and blue as though washed and cleaned of all its winter clouds in honor of the coming Passover. Cloudlets of transparent azure bathed in the joyous light, and the red-gold sun shone behind the Breslaw forest sending his golden beams through the naked twigs of the trees. A flock of black crows flew after the travellers. Finding no place to rest, they hovered above the sleigh,

98 KIDDUSH HA-SHEM

descending now and then, and lightly touching the
snow where they left imprints of their feet. A violet
red color hovered in the air, compounded of the whiteness of the snow and the blue of the sky.

The damp odor of decayed roots and of the primi-
tive naked soil hung in the air. Occasionally the
sleigh passed through a field of snow where the foot-
prints of wolves could be seen, and every time it
came upon these sharply-outlined foot-prints, a voice
was heard from the sleigh:

"Hillel, we are in the bare fields among wild beasts,
and night is falling, Hillel."

"We'll arrive soon, master dear. You can see
the church spire of Breslaw already."

"What good is the church to me, Hillel? We have
to say afternoon prayers and it is getting late. And
it is dangerous to stop in the field."

"We'll arrive soon, master dear."

"We'll be late for the Eighteen Benedictions, Hillel."

"We'll not be late for the Eighteen Benedictions,
God forbid. We'll get there even before afternoon
prayers."

And Hillel began to urge his horses in all the different
languages that he knew. He spoke to them in Russian,
"Get up, little brothers, get up!" He spoke to them
in Yiddish: "Dear little brothers, do hurry up a bit,
the master has to say afternoon prayers." But they
understood best when Hillel began to sing a portion
of the morning service. Hillel gave free rein to his
voice across the bare fields. The horses fell into a
trot upon the fresh, damp earth, the road receded

beneath their feet, and soon they entered the muddy streets of Breslaw.

In the court-yard of Berachiah's tavern in Breslaw a large number of vans and sleighs were assembled. The inn was filled with Jews from the entire region. Many were on the way from the fair and intended to use the ferry for crossing the river to Nemirov. But the ice had already loosened, and huge lumps of it were sweeping down the river. Many Jews, therefore, from all the neighboring settlements were gathered in Berachiah's inn, waiting to cross the river.

Mendel found old acquaintances: Reb Gedaliah of Chihirin, Reb Yechezkel of Kolnik and Jews from Nemirov; also Reb Yoneh the Preacher, Reb Mosheh of Nemirov and many other Jews. They were all in jolly mood, well-disposed, and Chaskel Boruch, the liquor dealer, slapped Berachiah on the shoulder and shouted:

"Tell your wife to cook *kliskes* for supper!"

"And stuffed tripe," added Yochonon Aaron, the fisherman of Nemirov.

"With renderings of fat!"

"And *tzimmes*, even as for the Sabbath."

But there was no need for all that. At the large oven stood the innkeeper's wife, cooking the supper in a huge kettle over a lively fire. And the appetizing smell of the tripe and the stuffing and of the *kliskes* already pervaded the room.

"What is the great occasion?" asked Mendel.

"Nothing, just so. 'When the month of Adar

arrives, it is a duty to rejoice.' That's what we are Jews for! Isn't it a plain argument *a fortiori*? Since even the *Goyim*, who worship wood and stone, are rejoicing, how much more should we Jews rejoice, whose Father is the Lord of the Universe!" And Reb Chaskel of Kolsk, to emphasize his reasoning, poked his thumb into Mendel's beard.

"And have you said afternoon prayers, already?"

"Beginning with noon, and with the special Praise Service."

"What is the grand occasion?" asked Mendel, surprised.

"Simpleton, have you forgotten the year that we are in? We are in the year *Zos*, that is to say, *Tach**, and it has already begun."

"What has begun?"

"You have not heard? The wars of Gog and Magog, even as the holy Ari prophesied," Reb Yoneh imparted to Mendel.

"I come from Lublin and know of nothing."

"The wicked Chmelnitzki, the Cossack captain of Chihirin, has gathered thousands of Cossacks and is out near the Yellow River to fight the Poles."

"What's the news from Zlochov?" asked Mendel in alarm.

"Simpleton, it's the beginning of the redemption, the wars of Gog and Magog, and he goes about

---

* The year 5408, when these events are happening, is represented by the Hebrew letter-combination reading *Tach*, equal numerically to 408. The numerical value of the letters of the Hebrew word *Zos*, meaning *this*, is also equal to 408.

inquiring after Zlochov! Parnas, ignoramus!" and Yoneh turned from him and went into the next room, where a large number of Jews in prayer-shawls were assembled. Some were praying, others singing, still others engaged in study. Their exulting voices could be heard in the other rooms.

The frightened Mendel came in among the crowd and asked on every hand: "What's the news from Zlochov?"

"Don't worry about Zlochov! They are near the 'Yellow River.' The lords Pototzki and Kalinowski have assembled thousands of soldiers and gone out to give them battle." Reb Chaskel of Kolsk reassured him.

"God be praised," Mendel breathed again. "His end will be as black as Pawlick's a year ago. He will be beheaded in Warsaw," Mendel reassured them. "But still, why all this rejoicing?" Mendel inquired.

"Simpleton, that is just why we rejoice. The holy Ari prophesied this very thing, and there is a hint in the Torah that this year the Messiah will come. It can be seen as clear as daylight: '*Im tokum olai milchomoh be-Zos ani boteach*, if war should rise up against me, I am confident of *zos*. Now, what does *zos* mean? *Zos*, mathematically, means 408. That is to say, that in the year 408 a war will rise up against me—and I am confident of it—there you have it on the surface!" and Chaskel of Kolnik again poked his thumb into Mendel's beard. "And you, simpleton, go about asking why Jews are rejoicing! Ho there, Berachiah, tell your wife to put another tripe with

fat stuffing into the kettle and charge it to the parnas
of Zlochov!" Chaskel of Kolnik shouted to the innkeeper.

"And who is the lad?" Chaskel pointed to Shlomele.

"A married young man, returning from the yeshivah
of Lublin with a rabbinical diploma in his pocket.
My son, beshrew the evil eye."

"Your son with a rabbinical diploma in his pocket!–
A piece of pancreas into the pot and charge it to the
young benedict Reb Shlomo, son of Reb Mendel,
with the rabbinical diploma in his pocket!" Chaskel
again shouted.

"And afternoon prayers, have you already said
them? Where does one say afternoon prayers here?"
Mendel inquired.

"Prayers? This room is dedicated to eating.
Services are held in that one." Chaskel showed
Mendel the way.

Mendel was still in time for the last *kedushah* of
the afternoon prayers.

After evening prayers Berachiah set the table.
The room was already dark. From outdoors was
heard the sound of the ice-blocks sweeping down
the river. He lighted two pieces of kindling wood on
the oven, and several candles burned in the Sabbath
menorah. The drivers brought their torches of tarred
wood from the wagons and lighted them. The
tables and benches were all brought together, making
one large board. The men washed their hands and
seated themselves around the board. Berachiah's
wife brought the great bowl filled with stuffed tripe,

pancreas and liver, which emitted a heavy cloud of vapor. And Berachiah placed on the table a keg of brandy with a drinking cup. First of all, they took a few drops to drink their mutual health. Then they pulled the tripes out of the bowl, tore off pieces of it with their hands and treated each other. In the interval between tripe and brandy, they gave the cantor of Uman the honor of singing a piece, and he sang *Va-Yigdal*. Moreover, there happened to be among them a Jew from Uman, a musician, who used to circulate among the fairs and who played the violin very beautifully,—and he entertained the gathering with his playing. Also, there was among them an "ancient", one of the Cossacks, who played on a harp which the Jews had presented to him, he being very old. He used often to go out among the Jews, at Jewish weddings and on other joyful occasions, and afford the Jews pleasure with his playing and singing. And now he sang a beautiful song about an old king whom his children had cheated out of his crown and then exiled from his kingdom. And in the intervals between singing and playing, they spoke about the Messiah, about the Redemption which was near and about the wars of Gog and Magog. And later, when the gathering became a little hilarious, the women also came into the room. And because of their great happiness that the Messiah was at hand, they allowed themselves a liberty, and the women went through a very pretty dance. The musicians, together with the "ancient", furnished the music, and the Jews clapped their hands to the measure. And by reason of their great happiness and joy, some of the Jews forgot themselves, and taking hold of one end of a towel or cloth, they handed the other end to the women and danced with them.

And the old pious Jews sat and looked on and said nothing, for their happiness was very great, believing as they did that the Messiah was at hand.

Thus did the Jews spend the night in jollification. Many songs were sung and many stories of miracle and marvel were told concerning the Messiah, and many hidden meanings, Bible verses and mathematical problems were expounded on the subject of the year when the Messiah was due. And the "ancient", the harpist, also reported that there was much talk among the Cossacks that great events would take place that year. He had been to Kiev, and there had heard say that in the church the priest had found a document on the pulpit, sent down by their God, Jesus of Nazareth, warning them to prepare for that year....

In a corner near the wall sat three kabbalists, who shared neither in the feast nor in the general rejoicing. One was very stout, another was still a young man, the third was an old man. The stout one was fasting in order to make his body lighter. But he found this very hard, for his body possessed great vitality, and his soul often yielded to his big body. When the big pots with the tripe and lungs were brought in, he was unable to restrain himself, for his hunger became very strong in him. If he closed his eyes, his desire was stimulated through his nose and mouth, and he often opened his eyes and asked his neighbor:

"What is it they are eating there, hey?"

"Stuffed tripe," his neighbor replied.

"So!" he sighed bitterly, and in order to torment himself he looked straight at the food.

The old man had a gray beard, and the young one was very emaciated, nothing but skin and bone. They, too, were fasting and for a reason that no one knew. And the young man could not bear to see the rejoicing of the Jews. He jumped up and cried:

"Why do you rejoice for no reason at all? In the story of Esther is the word *Va-Tichtov*, and the letter TAV is written large; and the letter CHES of the word *Chur* is also written large. Now, what does that mean? That means that the edict of Haman has been postponed until the year TACH."

The people were filled with alarm and they looked to see who had spoken those words.

"Wicked one, you couldn't bear to see Jews rejoice. How abundantly do Jews worship the Lord of the Universe in sorrow, and now that, for once, they wish to worship Him in joy, you will not permit it!" the old man scolded the young one. "Rejoice, Jews, rejoice. It is written in the Torah: '*Be-ZOS yovo Aharon el ha-kodesh.*' what does that mean? That means: In ZOS, which is mathematically equivalent to the year TACH, Aaron will enter the temple. In the year TACH will come the great deliverance."

Shlomo looked at the old man and recognized him. It was the devout little tailor.

In the next room stood Jews with prayer-shawls drawn over their heads as on holidays, and sang aloud the *kedushah* with the melody which is used only on festivals.

CHAPTER TWO

SHLOMELE COMES HOME

At the door, mother and nurse waited for the young man coming home from the yeshivah. Neither his mother nor his nurse recognized him. Shlomele was very much altered, having grown into young manhood. His thin black beard was already sprouting and mingling with the long curled ear-locks. His beard added age to his features, and the mother had a feeling of respect for her son. The glory of the Torah rested on him and she was in doubt if she might say "thou" to him...And Marusha, who stood behind the mother, was wiping her eyes and sobbing:

"The calf is grown up and knows not the cow that fed him."

The finest room of the inn was set apart for the young couple. Two sleeping-benches, which the father had ordered from the cabinet-maker for the young couple, stood against the wall of the low-ceiled room, covered with bed-clothes half way up to the ceiling. The beds were separated one from the other and curtained off with green cotton hangings. A large box, re-enforced with iron bands and mounted on iron wheels, stood in a corner of the room. It was packed tight with clothing and underwear and jewelry. A leather belt was fastened to this strongbox, in order that, in time of sudden misfortune, in case a panic should arise, it might always be ready for the owners to harness themselves into it and drag it along with them. There was also a table for eating and studying, a wooden sleeping-bench, and a cradle stood ready for the child which would come. The cradle with its stand belonged to the "suit" of furniture which the father had ordered for the young couple. But the most important fixture of the room was the shelf of books. The books were considered the chief stipulation which was embodied in the contract of betrothal, and the father-in-law, the rabbi, took great care that this stipulation should be strictly observed. Books were more precious than jewelry,—than the dowry, even. And not with money alone was this wealth of books assembled. Long years of effort on the part of the rabbi, as well as the love and devotion of Mendel brought the volumes together.

Thus stands ready the nest to receive the young couple, but his mate has not yet come. In the house of her mother the young woman sojourned for six years, waiting for the day when her husband would return from the yeshivah, a great scholar like her own father. The husband is already returned and the young couple have not yet met. She is to stay in her mother's house until the day before Passover, when her mother-in-law together with her mother will lead her into the nest which has been prepared for her and her mate.

For the Great Sabbath, the Sabbath before Pass-

over, Shlomele was invited to his father-in-law's
board. On Friday evening, when after the bath
he came in for the Sanctification of the Sabbath,
dressed in his new, fur-trimmed coat which he had
brought from Lublin, he saw his young wife for the
first time. She was standing in the next room together with her mother, the *rebbetzin*, and was blessing
the Sabbath candles. Was that his wife Deborah?
He remembered her only as the child he had left
behind. And there, at the Sabbath candles with
her mother, stands a young Jewish princess, a tall
slender figure, covered with a silver embroidered
veil. The embroidered head-dress, studded with
jewels, rests on her high white forehead like a crown
for her slender girlish head. Her white delicate
fingers conceal her eyes and face, and he only sees
her young, supple figure standing proudly, like a
young cypress, over the burning candles. Now her
luminous transparent fingers spread apart, and between them are revealed two large, black eyes, which
gaze upon him in silence and deep longing and shy-
ness. His heart beats fast and a yearning awakens
within him. It seems to him that those eyes have
always been with him. He saw them in the long
winter nights when sitting over the Talmud in the
yeshivah. An eager tenderness takes possession of
him, and he gazes upon her, but unable to bear her
moist, yearning glance, he lowers his eyes. A moment
later he raises them again, but her eyes are now covered,
and he only sees her shining, ivory fingers and stands
lost in thought.

He is deaf now to the clever exegesis which his father-in-law rehearses. The young man is no longer thinking of Maimonides with whom he had planned to take by storm the fortifications which his father-in-law had so cleverly set up. He is now thinking of quite other things. Those eyes, those proud, black cherry eyes which peeped out between the slender fingers at candle-blessing, are now before him, and he remembers that he saw them very often through the years of his stay at the yeshivah. In the sadness of the twilights, when great shadows shrouded the walls and tomes of the study-hall, he saw those eyes. Even so did Rebekah gaze upon Isaac when he met her on the road. Even so Rachel gazed on Jacob when he came upon her with her sheep near the well. And even so does the Divine Presence gaze at the Lord of the Universe when, every fast of the Ninth of Ab, she visits the ruins of the temple and there meets her Friend, the Lord of the Universe, seated in deep sorrow; and two great tears flow down from His eyes and set the waters of the Jordan to seething. And even so gazes the Sabbath Queen when she descends from the heavens and comes into Jewish homes, the time when mothers bless the Sabbath candles.

And as the young man is thinking these things he suddenly perceives approaching from the next room a holy shape. He feels her steps coming nearer, though he does not see her. His eyes look down on the floor, but within him there is a sudden light and a shimmering as of silver.

In the doorway of the room stands Deborah.   He
has not yet looked into her face, but a bright silver
light is dancing before his eyes.

"Shlomele, your wife wishes to see you," says the
rebbetzin.

Shlomo opened his eyes and saw Deborah before
him.   They were alone.

Deborah was first to speak to her husband.

"Shlomo," she said, "When you left for the yeshivah I wept a great deal.   I did not want you to go
to the yeshivah, for I was a child and did not understand.   Wherefore, you had regard for my weeping
and did promise me something.   And now I have
come to ask of you if you have kept your promise."

Shlomo made no reply, but stepped up to the chest,
opened it and said:

"Here you have that which I did promise you."

The girl remained standing before the chest in
wonder and amazement.   The golden slippers
gleamed out of the chest.   She took them out and
examined the high heels made after the Warsaw
fashion, and the coat of Slutzk silk embroidered
with silver.

For a long time Deborah examined her husband's
gift.   Then she rose up from before the chest and
said:

"And so you did not forget me.   And even when
you were so far away from here and for such a long
time, you did, nevertheless, remember me and did
vouchsafe unto me your kindness."

"Are you not my wife, sanctified unto me in accordance with the laws of Moses and Israel?" her husband replied.

"I know not if I am worthy of being your wife, Shlomo. I am a sinful woman and do not know how to bear myself toward God and toward man. I am ignorant, and you are such a great scholar. In the yeshivah you acquired so much Torah, and among strangers so much refinement."

"God has gifted you with great charm, Deborah, even like mother Rachel," Shlomo whispered.

Deborah looked at him with her moist glance, which Shlomo was unable to withstand. For a minute she was silent, then she said:

"Even for this have I prayed God both day and night, that I may find favor in your sight. And now that God has heard my prayer, what more do I need?"

"What have you done all the time that I was at the yeshivah, Deborah?"

"Mother taught me how to be a good and pious wife, and your mother taught me how to bring up our children 'for the Torah, for the canopy and for good deeds.'"

Shlomo came near to her and touched her head-dress without looking at her.

"May God grant us happiness and joy all the days of our life, Deborah."

"Amen," she responded.

CHAPTER THREE

THE FEAST OF WEEKS

The beautiful holiday which commemorates the receiving of the Torah arrived, and with it came the spring to the steppe. Zlochov was inundated by a sea of moist, green, velvety grass, which streamed from the steppe into the town. The vegetation sprouted wherever it could get a foothold, and not only was the earth green with the moist plants but the roofs of the houses seemed to blossom, and even the walls. The houses looked as if they grew up out of the earth, decked out and beflowered as they were with the wild vine, which clambered all over the walls. And above the low roofs, spread the sheltering branches of the linden trees which bent towards each other, became entwined and hung over the houses like a canopy. Every gutter in Zlochov was transformed into a row of flowers, and every marsh was covered with forget-me-nots. Golden yellow daisies twinkled on the moss-covered roofs. Tall bushes of jessamine looked into every window of Zlochov, and the fragrance of white lilac filled the little rooms.

And the breezes of spring which came from the steppe began to sweep through Zlochov, blowing from the welling waters which had been liberated from the ice, winds from the great green sea, which flowed around Zlochov in waves of hills and dales of blooming

forests and flowered steppes. And the twilights
came when trees and shrubs became wrapped in
dark shadows, and Zlochov seemed threatened to
be wholly engulfed in the steppe and never more to
emerge from it.

The day before Shovuos, as the children of Zlochov
were playing at the log near the public well in the
market-place, there arrived in town a little old Jew
with a round white beard, a big sack slung over his
shoulder and a stick cut from a branch in his hand.
The children looked eagerly at the stranger, for it
was seldom that Zlochov had a visitor. Suddenly
a boy with curled ear-locks and bare feet jumped from
the log and cried:

"There goes the little tailor, there goes the little
tailor!"

The children recognized the little tailor and ran to
meet him, shirts and trousers askew, and faces smeared
over with the juice of berries.

"Little tailor, little tailor, Hurrah!"

"Keep away, away!" The little tailor waved his
stick.

"Come to my home, little tailor."

"To mine, to mine!"

"No, to mine! You will sleep on the sleeping-
bench."

But the little tailor had his own lodgings in town,
in the vestibule of the synagogue. The children
followed him gleefully. In the vestibule he put down
his sack and took from it gifts of all sorts for the
children. To one he gave a whistle carved out of a

twig; another received a honey-cake saved from the previous town; and a third, who was already able to read, got a little book. And, as there was still time before going to the bath, the children gathered around him and he taught them a fine song for the holiday.

At night after the services, the householders of Zlochov quarrelled as to which one of them should have the honor of entertaining the little tailor. Each of them was anxious to observe the sacred duty of hospitality, for it was very seldom that they had the opportunity of fulfilling this duty in Zlochov.

The first day of the festival he ate in Mendel's home, this honor being the special prerogative of Mendel, as parnas. At the table the little tailor was very jolly, he sang and talked, a thing which he was not in the habit of doing. He was greatly rejoiced over Shlomele because of the young man's return from the yeshivah of Lublin, and demanded tuition money from him for having taught him to read his prayer-book, and Shlomele rewarded him with a cup of ale. As the little tailor drank the ale, he sighed:

"Behold Zlochov grown to be 'a city and a center in Israel,' the pity of it!"

But no one understood his sighing and his "pity of it". They marvelled over it, but no one questioned him, for the ways of the little tailor were indeed wonderful.

Very early the following morning, the second day of the festival, Shlomele was sitting in his room studying his portion of the Talmud. The little

window was open, and the trees which grew behind
the window looked into the low-ceiled room. The
sweet singing of birds could be heard outdoors, and
a sweet scent of honey was wafted from the honey-
flowers of the steppe, and filled the low, little room
of the young husband and bride. The young wife
was standing over the chest and taking out her fine
dresses and jewels with which she decked and embellished herself to go to the synagogue with her
mother-in-law. A great charm rested on her that
spring holiday morning. Her cheeks were tender,
the bliss of the night still lingered on them, and her
large eyes were veiled with a brilliant dew as though
they were not yet awake from the dream of the night.
And a great love for his wife was kindled in the heart
of the young man, and he felt for her a great pity
and tenderness. And her heart also was filled with
love towards him, for his Torah chant that holiday
morning sounded as sweet in her ears as the singing of
happy birds. For they loved each other very much,
as is usual with young people just after the wedding.
And he could not continue his studying, so he placed
his fur hat on the Talmud folio, and paced up and
down the room. And she, his young wife, decked and
embellished herself before him in her finery. And
when she was very beautifully adorned, she rose up
from before the chest and approached her husband
that he might bless her before she set out for the
synagogue. And he laid both his hands on her
beautiful head and spoke as follows:

"May your loveliness remain ever with you as with our mother Rachel."

And the young woman took her large prayer book with the covers of silver which her father-in-law had given her, and with a great flourish, decked out in her holiday finery, she set out for the synagogue.

The people were gathered in the synagogue. The women, dressed in their holiday best, are standing in their separate section, and through the curtained railing look down into the section for the men. Between her mother and her mother-in-law stands Deborah, beautiful in her new, jewelled head-dress which her father-in-law had given her when she had presented herself before him in honor of the holiday, wearing the golden slippers which Shlomele had brought her from the yeshivah. She looks down through the railing and sees Shlomele, wrapped in a long prayer-shawl, standing on the pulpit, holding a scroll of the Torah in a loving embrace, and singing a song in glorification of the festival. Like a songbird he caresses with his sweet voice the melody of *Akdomos*, imparting to each word all the beauty of the chant. And as Deborah listens to Shlomele's voice, sweet thoughts come to her and course through her soul like music, thoughts that softly steal their way in and raise a tender blush on the young woman's cheeks and a moist, bashful look in her eyes. She hides her eyes in the palm of her hands as though afraid lest her mother read in her face the sweet thought that she is thinking.

Still as in a dream sounds the music of her husband's

voice, when a violent noise from the street breaks
in and drowns the holiday song. No one at first
dares put away his prayer-shawl and step out to
see what has happened. And Shlomele strives to
raise his voice and to add more sweetness to his
singing, but the tumult of the street comes nearer
to the synagogue and banishes the holiday. Here
and there, one and another slip out of the synagogue.
The parnas is banging on the platform table, and
the next minute a crowd of men, women and children
break into the synagogue and a murmur rises up:

"Messengers are coming."

"Two messengers from Karsoon."

"They've come on horseback; desecrated the holiday."

"It's a matter of life and death!"

No one now listens to Shlomele's trilling; the holiday song is silenced. Mendel is striking the platform
table, the people are running in and out of the synagogue.

All at once there is heard the sound of weeping.

"What has happened?"

"Silence! Silence!" Mendel strikes the table.

Just then the door of the synagogue is opened
violently, and a frightened voice calls out:

"Jews, flee for your lives!"

CHAPTER FOUR

THE EXILE FROM ZLOCHOV

On the synagogue platform, decorated with holi-day greenery, among the scrolls of the Torah in their mantles of silver cloth stand two Jews in their week-day clothes, covered with the dust of the road, who had arrived on horseback in despite of the holi-day.

The wicked Chmelnitzki has defeated the two Polish generals Pototzki and Kalinowski, the Jews report, and he is advancing with his armies on the whole of Ukraine. The Khan of the Tatars has joined him. The kehillah of Karsoon has already been utterly destroyed. Many Jews have perished. Only they, the riders, have saved themselves, and galloped to Zlochov, desecrating the holiday, in order to inform their fellow-Jews of Zlochov that the danger is very great, that despite the holiday they must flee for their lives, because Chmelnitzki with his Cossacks and Tatars is advancing on their city.

Thereupon a panic arose in the synagogue. Mothers snatched up their little ones and ran without knowing whither. Some shouted that the horses should at once be harnessed to the vans and all escape from the city despite the holiday. But no one dared do it. They could not imagine that their lives could be cut off so suddenly. No one found it in his heart to move a single object on that beautiful holiday. In the meantime more and more men, women and children came running to the synagogue, as if seeking a place of hiding in the House of God. No one remained at home, all felt that they must be together in the synagogue.

And Mendel the parnas, looking very pale, stepped up to the platform and striking the table, spoke as follows:

"Jews, let us not leave this place. We have built up a settlement, a synagogue—in whose hands are we going to leave all this? It can not be that a whole world should be destroyed. Another day or two and help will come. The lord Vishnewetzki will arrive with Polish soldiers, other nobles also. In the meantime we will hide, lock ourselves in the synagogue. And it may be that Chmelnitzki has turned aside with his armies toward Chihirin, where he lives. What has he against us? We have done him no harm. To take a city and destroy it deliberately, to abandon everything to rack and ruin —no, we will not go!"

Many were reassured by Mendel's words. The Jews who had been there from the beginning, when the settlement was first built, were so deeply attached to Zlochov that they seized upon the ray of hope which the parnas offered them in the possibility that Chmelnitzki had turned aside toward Chihirin because his home was there. The calamity befell them so suddenly, so unexpectedly, that they were unable to realize the danger. And soon there gathered round

Mendel a group of Jews, manual laborers, horse-dealers who used to travel about among the Cossack camps and trade with the Cossacks, often at the risk of their lives. They were men of strength and courage, their faces tanned by the sun of the steppes, with strong, black beards and bushy brows, Jews with broad shoulders and large, heavy hands,—hands that had built up cities. And they were in accord with the parnas.

"Whoever wishes to go, let him go. We stay with our parnas."

"We stay with our synagogue."

"The synagogue! In whose care will you leave the synagogue? The Cossacks will burn it!"

Silence fell upon the assembly. The rabbi arose, stepped up to the platform and struck the table:

"Jews must not risk their lives to no purpose. 'And thou shalt preserve thy life,' is written in the Torah. And he who destroys himself knowingly has no portion in the world to come. And the saving of life takes precedence over the Sabbath, even over the Day of Atonement. Therefore, as rabbi, I command the parnas of the community to be the first to harness his van and leave the city at once, for the danger is very great."

The parnas did not stir. He remained seated on the platform.

"Whoever wishes to go, let him go. I will stay here with the synagogue. God has built a synagogue and he will protect it. Abandon a city to rack and ruin,—I will not do it."

The people, seeing that the parnas stayed, were
in no hurry to obey the rabbi's command. Around
Mendel gathered the butchers, the horse-dealers,
the camp-traders, and no one dared to be the first
to desecrate the holiday.

A dead silence fell upon the synagogue. All looked
to see what the rabbi would do. The rabbi said not
a word, but stepped up to the Ark, took up two scrolls
of the Torah in his outstretched arms and started out
of the synagogue.

"Jews, save the Torah scrolls!" the rabbi said.

But he need not have said it. Seeing the rabbi
carrying the scrolls out of the synagogue, the people
broke into loud wailing. Only then did they realize
the catastrophe. They recalled the time when the
scrolls were installed, and they wept frantically. No
one could speak or think. The scrolls of the Torah
were taken up, and the people trooped out of the
synagogue after the rabbi.

Old Reb Shmuel was no longer alive, so another
Jew took his little scroll under his arm and left the
synagogue with it.

And the rabbi exclaimed:

"Jews, you may profane the holiday, I command it!
Harness your wagons and save whatever you can.
I will do the same."

The people hastened from the synagogue after
the rabbi. There was a running to and fro. Here
and there horses were being harnessed to the vans.
They pulled them up in front of the houses, helped
in the little ones, and began dragging out their be·

longings, especially books and bedding. Some pulled out of their houses the chests in which they kept their precious articles, harnessing themselves into the leather belts and dragging the trunks on wheels through the streets towards the cemetery. Others snatched up whatever first came to hand—a dish, a garment, a piece of furniture. Some still had on the prayer-shawls they wore in the synagogue. Thus the people of Zlochov followed their rabbi out of the city and on the road to Nemirov.

And on the platform of the synagogue still sat the parnas of the community, firm as a rock, listening to the stamping of hoofs and the grating of wheels. That was Zlochov on the run, Zlochov flowing out— and he stirred not from his place. Around him were gathered the laborers and horse-dealers, and all were silent.

Shlomele stood near his father. He agreed with the rabbi that the saving of life takes precedence over everything, and he begged his father to leave the synagogue and go with the rest. But his father continued to sit immovable as a rock.

"God built a synagogue, and He will protect it," he mumbled in his beard.

Seeing his father bent on staying, he stayed with him. And together with him were Deborah and the rest of Mendel's family. And the old Christian woman Marusha stood near the door of the synagogue and cried:

"Dear master, run away; the little brothers will

come from the steppe, they will spare no one. Save your life."

But no one noticed her, for she dared not go into the synagogue but stood near the door weeping to herself.

The noise and tumult outside began to subside. Zlochov became drained and empty. The steppe now won back the portion of which man had robbed her. The synagogue became silent. Cold draughts seemed to be wafted from its dark corners. Through the two little red-and-blue windows in the ceiling brilliant pencils of light entered and zigzagged across the synagogue, lighting up the open Ark and the stars which were painted on it. In front of the pulpit burned a solitary candle which the sexton had lighted for the holiday services. Around the railed platform still hung the rushes and other greenery, for it was the custom so to decorate the homes and synagogues in memory of Mount Sinai. On the platform sat the silent guard, the parnas and his companions, who remained with him to defend the synagogue.

Suddenly some one rose up from a corner and approached the platform. It was the little tailor. No one had until then noticed him where he sat in a corner, singing his Psalms. Mendel and the others were surprised to see him. The little tailor looked hard at them and then spoke as follows:

"You are guarding the synagogue? What will you defend it with? Force? Is God in need of your force? Is not a stone, a piece of wood stronger than you are? Does God lack force?"

No one answered him.

But suddenly, in the corner from which the little tailor had emerged, a pale flame was seen to shoot up. The fire seized upon the curtain which hung in front of the Ark near by. And the next moment the oil-soaked pulpit-stand was ablaze.

"Fire! Fire! The synagogue is burning!"

"Who did it?" And the men jumped up to run to the fire.

"Wait, I did it!" And the little tailor kept the people back. "When the Lord of the Universe wanted to banish the Jews from Eretz Yisroel, says the Talmud, they had all incurred the penalty of death. But God poured out His wrath upon stones and sticks of wood. He burnt the temple and saved the Jews. Are you going to be better than the Lord of the Universe? What is it that you were going to protect? Stones and sticks of wood! Save your strength; God will require your strength for a higher purpose, when the time will come and we shall be privileged. Save your lives, they do not belong to you, they belong to God!"

The Jews were awed by the voice of the tailor. One by one they began to slip out of the synagogue. Moreover, there was nothing left to defend. The curtains and furniture, covered with oil and tallow, burned like kindling wood.

"Better so! We've burnt it ourselves before the *goyim* could desecrate it. Come, brothers, let us harness our horses," the parnas cried, and together with the members of his family, he left the synagogue.

"Up, old woman, and help pack. It is getting late."

A few minutes later, Hillel pulled up in front of the inn, and out of the house they began to bring the books and the chests. It was high time, for the priest together with some Cossack peasants had slipped into the inn and were beginning to steal the liquor.

"I have always told you that the little brothers will come from the steppes. They come flying on swift horses and the Angel Michael accompanies them," the priest, already drunk and staggering, cried to Mendel with great cheerfulness.

"You hound's son," Marusha beat the drunken priest over the head with a slipper, "When the master is away the pigs crawl out of the sty."

And as the parnas's van was leaving the city, the last in the procession, Mendel turned and looked for the last time on Zlochov. He saw the synagogue burning alone and it reminded him of a candle that burns for one that is dead.

CHAPTER FIVE

"We Will Do and Obey"

Long caravans of covered wagons wound across the steppe, filled with women, children and bedding, converging from the entire neighborhood towards Nemirov. At night, afraid to proceed on account of wild beasts, they halted near a river. The women and children fell asleep and the men mounted guard in order to protect the wagons against wild beasts and wicked Tatars.

They built a fire, and the old Jews sat around it, devoutly chanting Psalms, while the younger men stood guard.

It was the night of the second day of the festival of Shovuos, when Jews ordinarily rejoice in the Torah. The pious little tailor would not allow the people to fall into melancholy.

"Jews, let us rejoice in the Torah!"

The people made no answer. Each one was preoccupied with his own affairs. Their grief in having left their city was very great, and they forgot the holiday, they forgot their faith in the Lord of the Universe. And that was why no one answered him.

"Poor Jews,—at the very first trial you lose your faith," some one remarked.

"And perhaps this is His way. He wants to see

the Jews rejoice in the Torah, not in the houses of cities or in synagogues, but in the open field."

"And the Jews who received the Torah from Mount Sinai had no cities or houses either, and no synagogues as yet. They were encamped in the open field even as we are, nevertheless they said: 'We will do and obey.'"

"We will do and obey!" some one exclaimed.

And it was as if a great consolation had come upon the people, as if a spark of hope had kindled their hearts and caused their faith to blaze up. They began to understand, to perceive the reason of it, and soon one of them took out the little scroll, the Zlochov scroll which accompanied the Jews into exile, and exclaimed in a loud voice: "We will do and obey!"

And the people responded lustily:

"We will do and obey!"

Some one began to sing the Psalms from the Praise Service, and the people after him. The children woke up and saw the great fire burning in the steppe and the Jews dancing around it with their scrolls.

"We will do and obey!"

And the steppe was transformed into a Mount Sinai—loud the fire crackled, and far and wide resounded across the steppe the cry of the Jews, dancing with their Torah scrolls around the fire:

"We will do and obey!"

In a few days they reached Nemirov. The city was full of newcomers, Jews from all over the region, who had fled thither to take refuge in the fortified city against Chmelnitzki's Cossacks. The Kehillah of Nemirov, with its parnas, Reb Yisroel, and its rabbi, Reb Yechiel Michel, at the head, did for the refugees everything they could. The new-comers were housed in the synagogues, the women and children in the women's sections. And the charitable women of the city collected bedding and clothing and arranged comfortable beds for the women and children. In the synagogue court off the Jewish street, fires were blazing beneath great kettles of food for the hungry. Whoever had a relative or an acquaintance, near or distant, sought him out, and soon Nemirov became one large community. Both the residents and the newcomers slept in communal houses and ate together out of the com-munal kettles.

The news came that Chmelnitzki had turned aside to capture Chihirin, his own city. There he had massacred the entire Jewish community, with Reb Zechariah at the head, upon whom he inflicted terrible tortures before putting him to death. Reb Zechariah and the entire community of Chihirin died for the sanctification of His name as befits Jews. They put on their praying-shawls and white robes, and assembled in the synagogue, where they all perished. The news also came that Chmelnitzki had burnt several Jewish settlements, among them Zlochov. But they still had confidence in Prince Vishnewetzki who was advancing with a large army from the other side of the Dnieper to give Chmel-nitzki battle. So they waited for Prince Vishnewetzki,

who was also a great friend of the Jews, to defeat
the wicked one, so that the Jews might return to their
ruined settlements.

But it soon became known that Chmelnitzki defeated the noble friend of the Jews. Prince Vishnewetzki retired to Lithuania, and the entire country
was left without any defense, abandoned to the enemy.
Nor could they expect any help from Warsaw, because after the death of king Vladislav, the nobles
could not agree as to who should be chosen king of
Poland. And the kingdom of Poland was left like
a ship without a rudder.

So the rabbi of Nemirov, Reb Yechiel Michel,
called a meeting of all the parnasim and other
notables who happened to be in Nemirov, in order
to take counsel together on what they should do,
for the danger was very great indeed.

At the meeting there were differences of opinion.
Some held that they ought to leave the city and move
on to Tulchin, which was a stronger fortress, Others
urged that they remain where they were. Among
the latter was the parnas of Zlochov, who spoke as
follows:

"Whither shall we go? Whither shall we flee? A
whole country of Jews are going to flee! And where
are we going to stop? And will they not come to
Tulchin also? If, God forbid, no help should come,
they are sure to conquer the entire country as far
as Lvov, as far as the Vistula. But it is impossible
that Poland should perish. The nobles are not going
to allow their own cities and villages and property

to be burned. Help is bound to arrive. How can a whole country be abandoned to destruction?"

They all listened to the words of the parnas of Zlochov, and agreed that there really was nowhere to flee; that if Nemirov, with its rabbis and parnasim, with its stalwarts and its large assemblage of Jews, should have to flee, then it was really the end of the world. And, they agreed, it was impossible that the nobles would abandon the whole of Ukraine to the enemy.

"But what shall we do?" the Jews asked.

"Nemirov has a fort. On one side there is the river, on the other sides the walls. We number, thank God, several thousand Jews here in Nemirov. To begin with, let us intrench ourselves in the fort so that the Russians who live here and the Poles may not be able to surrender it to the Cossacks when the latter reach the city. And we will defend ourselves until help arrives from Poland. It is impossible that a Government should allow an entire country to perish."

The plan pleased them all, and it was agreed that they should follow the wise counsel of the parnas of Zlochov.

Only in a corner of the meeting room sat the little tailor and mumbled fiercely to himself: "Force! Do they wish to help the Lord of the Universe with their force? Save your strength for yourselves. A time will come when you will need your strength for yourselves, for a higher purpose!"

But no one paid any attention to him. The small

town parnasim who were assembled at the rabbi's, were all of them Jews in the same position as Mendel. They had themselves built the towns of which they were the leaders, and because they loved the towns from which they came and were unwilling to abandon them to ruin, they all concurred in Mendel's advice and began at once to carry it out.

On one side of Nemirov flows the river, and a stone rampart enclosed the other three sides of the city. On the corners of the walls stood high stone bastions which had a number of old rusty cannon. But there was no ammunition and no one knew how to operate them. But the Jews had no thought of shooting, but only of how to fortify themselves. So they began by strengthening the gates of the wall. The Jewish blacksmiths forged long iron bands, bolts and iron chains with which they strengthened the gates. And about the walls they set up scaffolds with ladders, and built a wooden fortification on which they assembled heaps of stones, sharp poles and cauldrons of boiling water.

There were also in the city several hundred Poles and a number of German artisans who knew how to use fire-arms. But the Jews were not willing to trust them with the walls or the bastions. They were willing to let them stand on the scaffolds and help repel the Cossacks when the latter arrived. The first thing the Jews did was to hide the girls and young women and their precious possessions in the bastion, and they themselves mounted the walls.

Nemirov became more and more crowded. **More**

and more Jews arrived from the small towns, and they brought the woeful tidings that Chmelnitzki had sent out his general Krivonos with a large number of Cossacks and Tatars who were advancing on Nemirov. A great fear fell upon the Jews. And the rabbi, Reb Yechiel Michel, assembled the people in the Nemirov synagogue on the Sabbath and he put on his prayer-shawl, and stood up to address them.

"My masters, we do not know what is in store for us," said the rabbi. "A serious time for Nemirov is approaching. The Lord of the Universe desires perhaps that we die to sanctify His Holy Name. In that case, we are prepared and ready. Perhaps the enemy comes to conquer not our bodies but our souls. For our bodies we have prepared a defense, we have fortified the walls. Have we also prepared a defense for our souls? If the wicked one should come and say: 'Give ye unto me your souls and I will let you live,' will you be strong enough to have no pity on your lives, on your wives and your children, and die for His Holy Name as did the Ten Great Martyrs, as did all the holy and the pure?"

The synagogue became silent. The women ceased their sobbing and the men their groaning. There could be seen only shining eyes and pale, mute faces.

And one of the people exclaimed:

"'Hear, O Israel, The Lord our God, the Lord is One!'"

And the people after him exclaimed as one man:

"'Hear, O Israel, the Lord our God, the Lord is One!'"

The rabbi was silent. He no longer spoke of martyrdom. His voice became softer, and he began to comfort the people:

"And this, perhaps, is only a trial. And you must remember the commandment: 'Thou shalt preserve thy life.' Every Jew is in duty bound to save himself as best he can. And he who takes his life with his own hands is guilty of the sin of 'destroying himself knowingly,' and has no portion in the world to come. You must not linger for anything, neither for possessions of gold and silver, nor, even, for holy books. For you do not belong to yourselves but to the Lord of the Universe, and you shall not risk your lives for anything but for the Holy Faith alone."

. A loud weeping arose in the synagogue when the rabbi was done. Families assembled together, each family, husband, wife and children, sitting separately, saying farewell to each other and comforting each other. And the faith of the people became stronger for the words of the rabbi.

———

The following day, the sentinels on the bastions saw a great cloud of dust rise up from the steppe. So they descended and brought down the black tidings that the wicked ones were coming. At once the men came running and took their posts on the scaffolds near the walls, armed with stones, axes and crow-bars, which they had assembled on the rampart, and the women brought kettles with boiling tallow and hot ground cereals which they had made ready. Then there hastened up Pan Kashnitzki, who was Prince Vishnewetzki's representative in the city, together with a number of Poles, sword in hand, and he cried to the Jews:

"What are you doing? For whom are you preparing the stones and heated cereals? For the soldiers of Prince Vishnewetzki, who are coming to save you from the Cossacks? Do you not recognize the white Polish Eagle on the red flags? Do you not recognize the tufts of peacock feathers on the heads of the soldiers? Are the peasant Cossacks dressed in royal ermine jackets? And are you not able to see from the distance the heavy ear-to-ear mustaches, not the drooping lobster-feelers of the Cossacks? Open the gate for the heroes of Prince Yeremiash, and go out to meet with honey-cakes and pearls the heroes who come to save you and your wives and children from the Cossacks!"

And, in truth, there was seen emerging from the cloud of dust a forest of flags on which the white Polish Eagle glistened in the sunlight. Here and there fluttered white flags in advance, as though bringing tidings of help and deliverance. And soon the entire rampart resounded with one shout of Joy:

"Help is here! Help is here!"

The women came out of the fortress with the little ones in their arms, clambered up the ladders and on to the walls, and, seeing the Polish flags in the distance, they cried:

"A miracle from God! See, see what God sends down from heaven!"

And the people of Nemirov came out on the streets, came out from the most secret hiding-places, from cellars and holes. Whoever had hidden for fear of the Cossacks came to the gate of the wall to see the arrival of the Polish soldiers who had come to their rescue. Here and there were assembling deputations of Jews, dressed in their holiday clothes, and carrying Torah scrolls, in order to welcome the soldiers of the Prince. Mothers were hiding their daughters for fear of the soldiers who were coming.... And youths and boys gathered on the wall to see the heroes march in.

The soldiers are already near the wall, but the Jews are in no hurry to open the gate. A herald with a white flag comes riding in advance, and after sounding his bugle calls out:

"Open the gate for the soldiers of Prince Vishne-wetzki!"

"Stand aside, Jews, stand aside! Open the gate, Polish soldiers are coming," shouts Pan Kashnitzki.

"We shall see. When they reach the gate we shall see what sort of soldiers they are," the Jews at the gate answered.

The soldiers are in no hurry to advance to the gate. The army is still at a distance, having halted in the little wood behind the city. They continue sending heralds with buglers, but the Jews refuse to hear of anything.

"We don't know what sort they are. Let them come closer to the gate and we will see what kind of soldiers they are."

"Ah, little Jews, cowards, how afraid you are! Open the gate and let me out to them. If I do not return—if those are Cossacks—it is my death. If I return, they are Poles. I do not need any of you. I alone will risk my life, and do you go and hide behind your women's skirts!" The Polish nobleman taunted them.

The Jews opened the little door in the gate and let Pan Kashnitzki out. The herald conducted the Pan to the army halting in the wood. There the Pan stayed a long time. Then he returned, mounted on a white horse and carrying a Polish banner. On either side of him was a bugler. The buglers blew a blast and the Jews stationed themselves on the rampart. The Pan read from a paper in a loud voice.:

"In the name of his Excellency, the Prince of Russ, Yeremiash Vishnewetzki, the Lord and proprietor of Nemirov, I command the inhabitants of Nemirov to open the gate for the soldiers of his Excellency."

"Long live our protector, Pan Vishnewetzki!" the Jews responded, and opened wide the gate.

The deputations ranged themselves in order. From the little wood the soldiers dashed forward to the gate helter-skelter, waving their banners in disorder and shouting "Hurrah!" The Jews were frightened.

Not in this manner does a friendly army enter its own city. But it was already too late. The first horsemen were already in the city.

By their long, drooping mustaches, like the feelers of lobsters, the Jews recognized them, and a terrible cry rose up in the city:

"The Cossacks! The Cossacks!"

CHAPTER SIX

NEMIROV

> "All this is come upon us, yet have we not
> forgotten Thee, neither have we been
> false to Thy covenant."   (Psalms)

A panic broke out in the city. The men snatched up whatever came to hand, the women caught up their little ones in their arms, and everybody ran. But whither to flee they did not know. Some cried: "To the cemetery! The rabbi has gone to the cemetery. If we must die, then let us be buried in Jewish graves." Others cried: "To the river! The rabbi ran to the river." But the Cossacks were already close behind them. In the streets were heard cries of terror of young voices, of maidens and young women whom the Cossacks caught up on their horses. Here and there a cry burst out and ended abruptly. And soon a dead silence reigned over all except for the dull thud of horses' hoofs.

The narrow streets of Nemirov became silent and empty as if all the inhabitants had died out. The streets were strewn with torn leaves of books, stained garments, fur hats, head-dresses, household utensils, broken brass candlesticks, strips of prayer-shawls and bodies of human beings. It was difficult to tell which was a body and which was a garment. Everything was jumbled together, beaten into one mass by the horses' hoofs. From the closed and shuttered little houses were heard frantic cries, cries of young and old and of little children that were abruptly cut off, the rattle of the dying and the long, long cries of young and strong voices. Occasionally a Cossack appeared coming out of a house half naked, his shirt torn and carrying in one hand a silver or brass candlestick and under his other arm a young girl, half naked with hair disheveled. The girl, straining to free herself from the Cossack's grasp, struggled and beat him on his naked back with her fists, which made the Cossack curl up his lips and laugh. Another Cossack came out of a second house carrying another girl who was half dead and lay unconscious across his bare broad shoulders. And both Cossacks stopped, laid their victims on the ground at their feet like bound calves, and exchanged girls, making up the difference in value by paying one another silver candlesticks, pieces of silken cloth, garments, boots or fur coats. Having made the exchange they parted, each one dragging away his victim. From another street appeared three drunken soldiers, half naked, with shaven heads and long twisted pigtails protruding through their sheepskin caps across their foreheads, their faces and bodies dripping with perspiration in the blazing sun, and carried on their backs naked children, some dead and some still alive, and called out in the streets, mimicking the Jewish butchers: "Fresh veal, twelve *groshen* a pound! Kosher killed, Kosher!"

But soon silence intervened. The cries of terror

in the closed houses ceased, except that from time to
time, in some remote street, a hue and cry arose
suddenly and grew still just as suddenly. In the streets
of Nemirov wallowed drunken, half-naked Cossacks,
wrapped in women's silken shawls and Jewish fur
coats. Some were covered with torn prayer-shawls
and strips of silken cloth. There lay about naked
Jewish women, girls, children, dead and living,
shattered chinaware, broken articles of ritual. Here
and there were strewn about torn parchments of
Torah scrolls, leather bindings of books, kegs of
liquor, tin plates with trampled food, weapons, pieces
of Turkish carpets mingled with human blood and
spilled liquor. It was impossible to tell who was
dead and who was alive. All seemed drunk, both
the living and the dead.

The hot summer day dragged on and on. It
seemed as if it would never end, and that the terrible
dread would last forever. Outdoors, the hot, bright
day illumined all things. But finally shadows began
to creep up from the steppe and the night began to
weave its dark pattern from house to house. And
soon all things were covered with the blackness of
night. Silence and blackness all about, and the stars
on high, and a buzzing and croaking from the marshes
as on every other night. Only the silence of death
hung over the black little houses. And in the midst
of it all, some one strummed on a lyre and sang a song
bewailing some one's dark fate.

In the city cemetery there was a stirring in the stillness of the night. From behind the headstones living corpses began to emerge. Some were wrapped in prayer-shawls, others were dressed in their long white prayer-robes, and still others who had had no time to seize their burial garments, hid in the cemetery, with the one thought of dying in the Jewish cemetery, where they would obtain *kever yisroel* among Jews. All day they waited for death, but death did not come. From the city they heard the terrible cries of the tortured, and they pronounced in a body the prayers of the dying when they confess their sins. And each one sought out the grave of his nearest and dearest and lay down waiting for death. But the day passed, and no one appeared from the city. The cries in the city came to an end. Then a hope was born in the hearts of the living. They found the courage to creep out from behind the headstones and one corpse began to speak to another.

"Praised be God, it is the end of the month, and there is no moon. It is a dark night."

"Will they go away, perhaps?"

"Is there any help?".

"Sh–sh–sh...."

Many had provided themselves with burial-clothes, and before running to the cemetery, had taken them along and put them on for two reasons, first, to make the Cossacks, if they should come, take them for corpses, and second if, God forbid, they should be doomed to die, they might be buried in their own burial-clothes. And now, in the night, among the head-stones, they looked like corpses which had clambered out of their graves and were wandering about among the living. Occasionally such a "corpse", dressed in burial-clothes, made its way into a group of living persons to beg.

"Who has a morsel of bread? I am starved," begged an old woman in burial-clothes.

"She is wearing her burial-clothes and is thinking of food," some one remarked.

"How can we help it? As long as the soul is in the body we must have food," replied the old woman.

Among the different groups there was also Mendel with his family. When the calamity struck, he, like other Jews, intended to get across the river with his family and escape to Tulchin. But when they saw the panic and havoc near the river, they concluded that they were doomed in any case, so they ran to the cemetery in order to die among Jews. All day the family remained together waiting for the death which they expected any minute. They said farewell to each other, and together pronounced the confessions of the dying. And Shlomele, who was a great scholar, comforted them and gave them strength. He assured them that they would enter straight into paradise, where those who die for His Holy Name are at once admitted. And he gave them a description of paradise with all its degrees and attributes, the sun of seven-fold strength, and the Heavenly Court with its eternal peace, where the

righteous sit with crowns on their heads, and the
angels play on golden harps and the Lord of the
Universe studies with them the Torah. He was more
familiar with the other world than with this. In
the sacred books of homilies and in the books of
kabbalah he had learned concerning the great and
holy life of the other world, where the Patriarchs and
the holy ones of all generations are to be found.
And what was this world with its terrors, with the
dominion of the wicked, compared with the great
and everlasting benefits of the world eternal?

With his words he lifted the spirit of his father and
mother and young wife, and prepared them for the
great trial which awaited them. They became calm
and were happy that they had with them their son
as a guide and comforter in their great extremity.
They forgot the anguish of death, they were freed
from the terrors of the world, and seeing only the
great and profound peace which awaited them im-
mediately after death, they looked forward to it as
to a great deliverance.

And under a headstone sat the young couple,
Shlomele and his wife. The night enfolded them.
In the heavens the stars shone big, and from the bank
of the river behind them in the valley rose the tumult
of the Cossacks. A shot rings out, little fires
flicker and become extinguished, and occasionally
a stifled sob breaks through the night. The girl
clung fast to her husband. It was not death she
feared, but parting with the joy she had begun to
feel; and closer and firmer she clung to him as though

she wished to die near him and together with him, that they might never be separated.

"Shlomo, we have just begun to live and we must part. God has not privileged me to be the mother of your children."

"Deborah, we have been united by God. He will bring us together again when we shall have the privilege of appearing before Him in holiness and purity. There, in the Heavenly Court, we shall be together forever, and delight in the glory of the Divine Presence until the Messiah will come, until the trumpet of the Messiah will awaken us for the resurrection of the dead."

And all at once their anguish became transformed into a great joy. They knew not themselves how it came about. They felt that a great Sabbath was descending on the world and that they were entering into it with immense joy. And by reason of their joy, they recovered the power to shed tears, which they had lost because of the anguish of death, and the young woman said with a radiant smile which shone through her tears:

"When you speak, I find it so easy to die, Shlomo. Why do they not come and release us? I would find it as sweet to die as I should find it sweet to go with you to the marriage canopy."

"Say not so, Deborah. As long as we live, we must pray for life, not for death."

"With the dear God all things are possible. Yes, Shlomo, we shall live. I do so want to live for you, for you, Shlomo, so that I may have the great privilege, Shlomo."

"Be still, little Deborah, be still."

"Oh I do so want to live with you together,—in this world or in the next. Oh, to live and to know that you are with me." And the young girl fell sweetly asleep in his arms.

Shlomo sat near her and gazed at her. Her delicacy and beauty made his heart tremble. It seemed to him he no longer knew her. She seemed divested of all things earthly, she became as light, as ethereal, as one of the daughters of heaven, as one of the holy Matriarchs, as that divine feminine, the Divine Presence, that weeps in the night on the ruins of the temple, as the dove that symbolizes the People of Israel.

CHAPTER SEVEN

ACROSS THE RIVER

The night brought the will and the hope to live. Mendel abandoned the thought of dying. All his eagerness and energy were awakened. His shining eye looked keenly about, and all could read his thoughts. He was looking at the sleeping Deborah.

Deborah was young and beautiful, and if the Cossacks should capture her, they would spare her life and do her evil, which is worse than death. No one spoke of it but all were aware of it and thought of it.

In the meantime the people began to stir. Here and there little groups were formed, talking low and whispering. This gave Mendel even more energy. He rose up from his place.

"What are you going to do, Mendel?"

"I'll go to the fence and look—perhaps—"

"Mendel—"

"Hush-sh..."

"Where are you going? I'll not let you," his wife held him, "If we must die, let us die together."

"I'll go to the fence, perhaps there is hope..."

Deborah awoke. She looked about her frightened and asked:

"Who is playing so beautifully? I heard music in my dream."

And, in truth, the sound of a peasant's lyre was heard in the distance. It was playing a sad, weeping melody. A dread fell upon the Jews. Some said the Cossacks were coming, and the people fled among the headstones holding their breath. The mothers covered their children and warned them not to cry. Soon there was total silence in the cemetery. The only sounds heard were the trembling of the lonely willows aloft in their long branches and the song of the lyre, which came nearer and nearer.

At last some one came into the cemetery. The playing stopped and a Jewish voice called out:

"Jews, Jews, 'it is a time to act for the Lord.' What are you waiting for?"

The people found courage to rise and come nearer to the stranger. By the light of the stars they saw an old beggar with a lyre in his hand.

"Who are you?"

"You don't recognize me? Why, I'm the little tailor. I can speak Russian, so I disguised myself as one of their 'ancients', and am living among them. Now you must save your lives. I heard them say that in the cemetery there are many Jews with much gold and silver and that at daybreak they will come here. You must flee for your lives."

"Whither?"

"The river is calm, the blackguards are making merry in the city, guzzling and committing all manner of evil. Woe to the eyes that look upon it. Whoever is able, let him escape across the river, for the danger is very great."

The people began to move about. From behind
the headstones black shadows began to gather,
murmuring and moaning.   Suddenly there was a
running to and fro. Here and there were heard
sudden cries and groans.

"Hush-sh—they will hear you," several warned
the others.

"What are you doing? The *goyim* will see you!"

"Singly, singly...scatter over the field," some
one commanded.

And here and there some one crept by and slipped
out.

But Mendel remained sitting, looking intently at
Deborah without stirring.   He was pondering deeply.
They all knew what he was thinking of, and Deborah
also knew, and sat silent like one guilty.

The cemetery became more and more deserted, and
Mendel still sat without moving.

Suddenly some one crept near to them, and threw
herself at Mendel's feet.

"Dear master, save yourself.   The night is dark,
run away."   And falling on Deborah's neck she began to sob: "Dear little daughter mine..."

Mendel and his family were surprised to see old
Marusha, the Cossack inn-servant. They forgot
their danger for a minute in their gladness at seeing
her.

"What are you doing here? Why are you not in
the city? They will do *you* no harm."

"What are you thinking of? Am I going to
abandon my masters and go and make merry with

the Cossacks? If we must die, let us die together.
With whom I have eaten my morsel of bread, with
them will I live and die."

"But how did you get here?"

"I followed you. Seeing my masters run to the
cemetery, I also ran. I feared you would drive me
away because I am of a different faith, so I lay quiet
as a cat under a stone and thought to myself: 'I'll
lie here and wait until the little brothers come, and
then I'll take my two little ones and protect them
with my body and say: You may kill me, but spare
my little ones.' Of a different faith, but still my
little children."

"Go back to the city. Don't you see? We are
in danger ourselves. Go back to your own people
or they will torture you like us."

"Dear little master, do not drive me away," the
woman implored. "I have served you faithfully,
and I love my little children. And I have come to
save Deborah. Here I have brought her Cossack
clothes, I will disguise her as one of our own. I
will say she is my daughter, and so the little brothers
shall not notice her; I will make her old and ugly.
You take the mistress and the young master and swim
across the river. Perhaps God will help you. Do not
take the young mistress. I know my little brothers,
the Cossacks. They scent a young woman miles
away as the dog scents the hare. And for a woman
they will leap into Hell, not only into the river.
I'll disguise her as a Cossack woman and take her
to a fisherman not far from here. We will say we

are peasant women. I will give him eggs and he will take us across in a boat. There on the opposite bank we will meet again. Or else, I will bring her to you in Tulchin, with the help of God. With me she is safer than with you. Like my soul will I guard her, like my life,—my chick, my little one."

For a minute hope blazed up anew in Mendel. He liked the woman's proposal. But he could not bring himself to part with Deborah, although he realized that she was safer with the Cossack woman than with him. The feeling of "dying together" was so strong in him that he only stood silent and thoughtful. No one dared say anything or give any advice. They all waited for the father to decide.

But Marusha did not let him think. Again she threw herself at his feet and prayed:

"Dear little master, save yourself. I was in the city, I saw what the little brothers did to the Jews. The little brothers of the steppe have become wild and forgotten God. Evil times have come. The Cossacks have forgotten God. Run, run away."

"Follow me. What matters it how death strikes us?" Mendel urged on his family.

They left the cemetery, which lay in the valley, and soon reached the top of the little hill. From this point they saw the encampment of the Cossacks lying along the river. The camp was lighted up by the fires which burned beneath the kettles, and here and there by torches. The Cossacks were not yet asleep. The sound of playing and singing or drunken cries arose from different points. Circles were formed around dancing couples. Occasionally, a shout burst forth throughout the encampment. All these things could be seen and heard in the space between the hill and the edge of the river.

Marusha threw herself at Mendel's feet.

"Dear little master," she implored him, "don't go there. You see what is going on. It is certain death. The little brothers will see us. They'll detect the young woman."

"We must separate. In any case, we are face to face with death. When day comes they will see us. Perhaps, if we will seek to save ourselves, God will help us as he has done up to now, and we will meet again in Tulchin. And if, God forbid, we are fated to die, then let us die for His Holy Name's sake," said Mendel to his family.

And Mendel embraced them and lifted up his eyes to heaven.

"Oh, Lord of the Universe, be our help!"

None of them wept. They embraced for the last time in silence.

"Say farewell to your wife, Shlomele. Perhaps God will help us if we separate."

Husband and wife remained alone for a minute. Shlomo stroked her hair and spoke as follows:

"Deborah, have faith in God, He can do all things,—even when the knife is at the throat."

She said nothing, but looked into his eyes.

"And we shall yet meet again, Deborah, because of your great merit, for you are one of the righteous, Deborah."

"Because of your great merit, Shlomo. And if, God forbid, we do not meet again, I will come before the Lord of the Universe in holiness and purity, even as you have taught me."

"Take heed to your life, Deborah, and place your hopes in God!"

"For the sake of our children which God will grant us," the young wife whispered. And that was her last word to her husband.

Husband and wife separated.

"May God reward you for the goodness which you show us, Marusha," said Yocheved to the Cossack woman. "In your hands I entrust all that is dear to me, my life and the life of my son. And may God reward you for what you are doing for us. I know not if I shall be able to reward you."

"Pray God for us and we will pray for you," said the old Cossack woman, and disappeared with Deborah among the bushes.

Another minute Mendel waited. The tears which only now were able to break through, were streaming down Yocheved's face. For a minute Shlomo listened to the rustling of the branches and dry leaves where his joy had vanished.

Mendel now said: "Come, in God's name."

And Mendel began to creep on all fours among the bushes and weeds down hill towards the river, and his wife and son after him.

For a long time they crept among the bushes and weeds. The voices of the Cossacks came nearer and nearer. Now they could hear their laughter and talk.

More than once they thought they were lost. But
God helped them, they reached the bank unobserved.
The tall weeds concealed them. The camp had now
become more quiet. The fires beneath the kettles
began to die out and the din to subside. The torches
on the wagons were still burning, and here and there
a Cossack was taking his horse to the river's edge to
water him. Mendel, with his wife and son, lay in
the weeds to one side and waited for the camp to
subside even more, so that none might hear their
splashing in the water. They were afraid to speak
to each other and lay there holding their breath.

"The Lord seems willing to help us," Mendel
whispered: "I will take your mother on my back,
and you, Shlomo, follow me. And if you should
grow weak, seize hold of me."

There were two quiet splashes one after another, and
two black spots began to move on the surface, dis-
turbing the silent ripples. The river gave a sudden
heave backwards, and soft waves, one after another,
began to lap the sandy beach.

On the bank a Cossack was lying on his saddle,
gazing at the big stars deep in the sky, and humming
a melancholy, monotonous tune. He was roused
from his waking slumber by the rocking of the wave-
lets on the beach. He looked around swiftly and his
keen eye at once espied the two little streams furrowing
the gently rippled surface of the river. His eagerness
conquered his sloth, the two feelings for a minute
waging war within him. He took up his spear. He

was already barefoot and the *Tammuz* night was warm.
There was a splash in the water.

In the midst of his exertions as he swam, Mendel
thought he heard the call of "Shema Yisroel". And
out of habit, Mendel, as he swam in advance with his
wife on his back, responded in a paroxysm of dread:
"Hear O Israel, the Lord our God, the Lord is One!"

And when he stopped on the other bank, he found
himself alone with his wife, and in the star-light he
perceived on the surface of the river a little stream
heading for the opposite shore.

CHAPTER EIGHT

THE CAPTIVE

"Thou sellest Thy people for small gain,
and hast not set their prices high."
Psalms.

"What have you caught, little brother Cossack?"

"A little Jew, a young one. I thought it was a girl, so it looked from the distance. Then I see it's a young man with trembling ear-locks," said the Cossack who had waited for him on the bank.

"What will you do with him?" asked the Cossack.

"I don't know. To kill him would be a pity. Here I went and got myself wet all for nothing."

"If you let him live, you'll have to feed him."

"That is true, too," replied the Cossack with a groan.

Near the Cossack lay Shlomo dripping and bent double. He heard the words of the Cossacks, but they no longer concerned him. He was ready to die, and was now saying to himself his prayer of last confession. For a minute he may have pitied his young life and regretted the happiness which he had only begun to enjoy. But he was so certain that he would meet Deborah in the next world, where they would live the great eternal life in everlasting peace, that he was happy to be now approaching it. And if he did regret something, it was that Deborah was not

near him and that they were not to die together.
The uncertainty as to what might befall Deborah
tortured him, as well as the thought that he was
separated from her at the last moment. But soon there
came over him the tranquillity of faith in God, who
sees and knows all things.

The Cossack was holding him by the coat, and
more Cossacks gathered around them. The night
was dark and calm. The steppe and the river merged
together and were lost somewhere in the night.
Only the bank of the river was lighted up with little
fires. One Cossack after another approached the
group. They were all eager to know what the Cossack
had pulled out of the river.

"Is she young or an old grandmother?" And one
of them took a torch and held it to Shlomo's face.
Seeing the long, trembling ear-locks on the pale
young face, they burst into wild fits of laughter.

"Ho ho ho! He allowed the Jewess to get across
the river, and fished out the Jew. Look, Cossacks,
see what he has caught. Just look at his catch.
Oh, you are a fine fisherman!"

The Cossack, a young fellow, with a good-natured
face and two keen little eyes, examined his victim.
He had already kicked Shlomo several times, not out
of viciousness, but in his perplexity at not knowing
what to do with him. At last he made up his mind.

"I'll baptize him and make a gift of him to the
Church. I'll earn a little merit before God for my
pains."

As he spoke, the Cossack took from around his neck

a little metal cross and brought it close to Shlomo's face.

"Pray to Christ, get on your knees before Him, and I'll let you live."

Shlomo did not answer him. He remained lying as before, all huddled together, with his face buried in his bosom.

"Get up, Jew," said the Cossack, lifting him from the ground. "Look here, now, I am going to do you a great kindness. I am going to induct you into the Holy Church and, besides, I am going to let you live,— just because the Cossacks laughed at me. Pray to God, get down on your knees before Him and kiss the cross, and say after me these words: 'In the name of the Father, the Son'.... Say them, accursed Jew, or I will kill you. As God lives, I'll kill you."

But as soon as the Cossack released his victim, Shlomo fell to the ground, buried his face in his hands and remained silent.

"You will not do anything with him. I know these young fellows. In Karsoon I captured one of them, a young handsome one, it was a pity to kill him. I was willing to give him my own daughter to be his wife. 'Get baptized,' I say to him, 'and I will let you marry my daughter. You will come with me to the camp and become a Cossack.' It was all in vain, I had to kill him. Tough leather, that lot. The rabbis cast a spell over them. The rabbis give them a certain red wine to drink when they circumcise them, and this red wine does not let them forget their faith. You will not do anything with him. Better kill him."

"Their rabbis give them blood to drink when they get circumcised, and the blood possesses such power that whenever they wish to change their religion, the blood comes and prevents them," said a second Cossack.

"It is said that they see a sort of light before they die. In the light they see their mothers, and this does not let them change their religion. But when their eyes are covered, they are unable to see the light."

"What's the difference? You will not do anything with him. Kill him."

"Give him to me!" begs another Cossack.

"What will you do with him?"

"I will make a present of him to my grandmother." The Cossacks laugh.

"Kill him, don't let him suffer. It's a sin to laugh at one of God's creatures," says an old man.

"You are right, little father, it's best to kill him," decides the Cossack who had captured Shlomo.

In the distance the playing of a lyre is heard. A little old man approaches the Cossacks, leaning on his stick and plucking at the strings.

"Ah, Cossacks, what are you laughing at?"

"Can't you see, old man? A little Jew has been captured and we don't know what to do with him."

"Sell him to Murad Khan. He buys up all the Jews. For an old one he pays a piece of silver and for a young one a piece of gold. You may even be able

to obtain, in addition, a kettle of Tatar beer to treat
your comrades with. A shrewd fellow, this Murad
Khan. A great heap of Persian carpets and Turkish
weapons will he get for the Jews out there in Turkey.
And our little brothers, the Cossacks, don't know how
to take care of what they have. They kill the Jews.
In Constantinople they fetch high prices."

"You speak wisely, old man. Our brother Cossacks don't know how to profit from what they have,"
another Cossack assented.

"Hey there, old man, take us to Murad Khan.
Where is he?" says the Cossack, seizing Shlomo
by the collar and dragging him along.

"You had better not hold him so, you must take
care of him. For a dead Jew Murad Khan will not
give you anything," says the little old man.

"Make him prance a little, like a young horse.
Give him some brandy to make him look livelier."

One of the Cossacks took a copper vessel filled with
brandy, applied it to Shlomo's mouth and forced
the young man, who was half dead, to drink.

"Hear, O Israel, the Lord our God, the Lord is
One!" Shlomo heard a voice in his ear.

As though in a dream, but roused somewhat by
the spirits, he looked around him and saw the little
old man who took his hand and said to him:

"What now, little Jew, are you asleep? Wake
up and praise God!"

The voice sounded familiar to Shlomo, very familiar,
but he could not remember where he had heard it.

They arrived before a large court-yard surrounded

by a fence. From the other side of the fence was heard a murmur of Jewish voices as of people praying aloud. On a carpet before the door of the court-yard sat Murad Khan, and near him burned a vessel filled with pitch. Before him on the carpet lay little heaps of copper and silver coins, various Turkish articles, carpets, objects of barter. Murad Khan, a sickly man, with a long drooping mustache and calm, lack-luster eyes, sat silent; near him stood two Tatars with covered heads and called out in Cossack language:

"Little brother Cossacks, bring your captives to Murad Khan. Murad Khan, the great merchant, is buying up slaves."

"Cossacks, Cossacks, Murad Khan pays for slaves with good Turkish money."

A small Tatar approached the group of Cossacks, looked Shlomo over, felt him, and pointed with his hand at two small coins.

"With a pot of Tatar beer," the Cossack haggled. The Tatar shook his head.

"Then I'll kill him,—as God lives, I'll kill him. If you give me a pot of Tatar beer to treat the Cossacks with, then well. If not, I kill him."

The Tatar approached Murad Khan who sat squatting on his feet, sorrowful and mute like one who is being consumed by some disease. His face was listless and his sad almond-shaped eyes were without expression.

Murad Khan shook his head.

"In that case, let us kill him and not sell him to the Tatars."

"Wait, dear little Cossacks, wait," says the old lyre-player, and coming close to the Tatar, he whispered in his ear and gesticulated:

"That captive, there, is a very important Jew. I know him, he is a rabbi. The Jews of Smyrna will pay a big ransom for him. A rabbi, that's what he is."

Again the Tatar approached Murad Khan and repeated to him what the old man had said.

Murad Khan nodded. The Tatar took a pitcher of beer, which stood near Murad Khan, and carried him to the court-yard among the captives.

From the other side of the fence was heard the singing of Psalms:

"The Lord is my light and my salvation; whom shall I fear?"

"Come, dear little comrades, let us drink," said the Cossacks, and sat down on the meadow to drink the Tatar beer.

"And you, lyre-player, play us something jolly, and sad also," some of them begged.

The Cossacks sat in a circle around the player. He took up his instrument, plucked at the strings, and sang to them the following in a strange medley of Hebrew and Polish:

> Oh Thou, *Ribbono shel olom*,
> Why dost Thou not notice,
> Why dost Thou not witness
> Our bitter *golus*, our bitter *golus*?
> Our bitter *golus* we shall vanquish,
> To our land we shall return!

Return to our land,
And there find our Lord,
And there find our Creator,
And there find our Redeemer.
To despair we all refuse
Our courage we'll not lose;
Our Mother redeemed shall be,
Our Home rebuilt we'll see.

Be ye wise, await the end!

Abraham, dear Abraham,
You, our first old man;
Isaac dear, oh Isaac dear,
Grandfather ours;
Jacob dear, oh Jacob dear,
You, our father:

Why don't you plead for us?
Why don't you plead for us?
Why don't you plead for us?
Before our Lord, our God?

Our homes rebuilt shall be,
Our land redeemed and free.
And to our land restorèd we
Our own, own land,
Our own, own land...

CHAPTER NINE

THE DICE

A little fire of twigs was burning in the steppe. Near the fire sat three Cossacks, haggling among themselves:

"I saw her first, therefore she belongs to me," one of them, an old man, said. His shriveled face was illumined by the blazing twigs, and his small eyes, which were imbedded in his big broad face like two raisins in a lump of dough, glistened in the dark. He bent down towards the girl, who lay a little distance away from them on the bare field, covered with a long, white, Cossack cloak. He tried to stroke her with his old hairy hand, but it was forced back by the hand of an old woman, who was kneeling near him in a crouching posture, watching over the girl.

"It means nothing that you saw her first when she was hiding in the jungle," said the second. "What you saw was an old donkey, and it turned out to be a pretty little filly. An old grandmother is what you saw, a little old Cossack woman, before we scared her out of the bushes. And then it was I who recognized in her the young Jew girl. I pulled the cloth from her head and washed from her face the mud with which the old witch had disguised her. You saw an old blind plug, a lame old donkey, that is what you saw, and I found a young eaglet, a little

dove. Well, now, to whom, does she belong, to me
or to you?" Thus did a young cossack blood argue
with the old man. The fire lighted up his full round
face, which looked out from his high fur cap. He
had a pair of black, childlike eyes, which looked out
good-naturedly, even in anger.

"And I say, all three of us found her, so she belongs to all three. That would be comradely and
in true Cossack fashion," said the third Cossack,
who sat near the fire. He did not excite himself,
nor shout, as did the other two, but spoke firmly and
with assurance. His two mustaches hung down over
his mouth like the two feelers of a lobster. He was
half naked, and the fire played on the copper color
of his skin. He was holding a lump of pork on a spit
over the flame. Drops of molten fat dripped into
the fire, and made it crackle noisily. The fire cast
a red glow on his copper-colored face, which now assumed an ashen hue. His elongated black eyes were
buried deep in the sockets. His face also was elongated, his cheek bones protruded sharply, and on his
chin stiff black bristles were scattered. His head was
shaven, and a long wisp of hair, which was left on his
forehead, came down across his cheek, and this lent
to his face a tense and mute expression, as though it
had never been visited by a smile.

"Belong to all three? Oh no, comrade, either to
one of us or to none," replied the young one.

"Ho there, little suckling, don't talk back to an
old Cossack. The times we live in!" the first old man
groaned.

"Otherwise, let us kill her," remarked the squatting Cossack.

"It would be a pity to kill her, dear little comrade," the first Cossack replied. "It would be better to bring her to the Tatars; the Khan hasn't such a one in his harem. He will give us a little bag of gold for her, and the gold we will divide up."

"And what else will you take to the Khan? Your own wife and daughters? Ah, the times that have come upon us! Cossacks have become the servants of the Khan. Chmelnik has sold us completely to the Tatars. A Cossack can no longer afford himself a pretty Jew girl. Everything must be taken to the Khan. No, dear little comrade, either she will belong to one of us or else let us kill her, rejoined the half naked Cossack, and saying this, he took out from his girdle a little bag and shook out of it some bone dice.

"Comrades, let us act like Cossacks, let us throw dice, and whomever the dice will indicate, to him she will belong. It will be his good fortune, and let there be no jealousy among Cossacks on account of a pretty Jew girl."

"Right! Spoken like a comrade and a Cossack! Whomever the dice will indicate, for him God intended her, and let there be no jealousy among Cossacks on account of a Jew girl."

The young Cossack stood in silent thought, and with his velvet eyes gazed at the white coat under which lay the victim.

"Give way, little brother; shall Cossacks fall out on account of a Jew girl? Whomever God will de-

signate, to him she will belong; and if not to you,
then you will be able to get other Jew girls, enough
to fill up your mother's stables. Krivonos will lead
us to Tulchin, where Jewish women from all of
Ukraine have gathered, and you will be able to pick
to your heart's content."

The young Cossack bent suddenly down toward
the fire, took the dice and threw them.

"Three, eight, five," they began to count.

"Six, three, ten."

"Good throw!"

"Five, eight, twelve," someone called out and laughed, and his laughter re-echoed in the night from the
edge of the field.

Under the white Cossack cloak lay Deborah, and
her shining eyes watched the game of dice by the
light of the fire. She knew that the game was for
her. She was the stakes. But not for a minute did
she despair. An inner assurance that God would
help her overflowed her heart. She believed in all
Shlomo had said to her before their parting, that God
would bring them together and that they would live
together again. In her extremity, she remembered
and longed for the happiness of the days when she
was together with her husband. In that remem-
brance she found calm, and believed firmly that the
time would come when God would deliver her from
all her troubles and restore her to her husband. And
this faith gave her strength to live.

Again cries arose near the fire.

"Three, six, five."

"Seven, three, eight."

"Ha, Ha, Ha!"

"Four, eight, twelve," a hollow voice laughed heavily in the night.

At this moment there suddenly rose up from the grass the black spot which was kneeling near Deborah, and which they believed had been silenced forever by the blow she had received from the Tatar Cossack.

"For your souls may you throw dice, for your mothers, but not for my eaglet, my little one, not for her whom I brought up with so much suffering, not for my precious own one," old Marusha cried to the Cossacks, and bending down to the young woman, she embraced her and comforted her.

"Precious soul mine, God will help us, you will see, God will send a fire down upon them. Ah, the Cossacks have become wild, forgotten their God, forgotten their own fathers and mothers, there is no fear of the king in them and they obey no law. Ah, God's anger will destroy you with thunder and with lightning! He will burn down the bridges beneath you. He will cause the earth to split open. You will sink down into Hell, you sons of dogs."

"Be silent, old witch, be silent, you, who have sold yourself to the devil."

"Let us cut her tongue out."

"No, rather the head, then you will not have to cut the tongue separately."

From beneath the white cloak the shining black eyes now looked up into the sky and into the stars.

They were full of the faith that there among the stars
sat He who knows and sees all.

Of one thing she was certain, that she did not wish
to die. She would live and fight for her life as long
as she would be able to, even as she had promised
Shlomo. Not for her own sake but for her husband's,
that she might be privileged to be the mother of his
children.

The Cossacks were throwing dice for the last time:
"Three, six, five."

There now came to her mind the morning of that
Shovuos festival before the great disaster, when the
green trees and meadows looked in through the windows of their little room. She sees him again sitting
over the Talmud, swaying over it, and studying aloud.
She hears his voice, and it rings in her ears like a song.
And she stands near the chest and decks herself out
for his sake, no, for the sake of God, in order to go to
synagogue—in the holiday jewels which he had
brought her from Lublin, and she approaches him in
her pretty head-dress, and he lays his hand upon her
head and looks deep into her eyes.

From near the fire there now sprang up a tumult,
clapping of hands, a wild, bestial laughter. She did
not understand what it meant, but she knew that the
crucial moment was at hand, and that now God
would help her.

From near the fire someone rose up. The silent
naked Cossack approached the white spot with shuf-
fling steps, and tore away the Cossack cloak. In
the starry night there was revealed a girlish body,

half wrapped in torn rags, which curled up and shrank into itself like a worm.

"You will not come near, you will not do my child evil, I will scratch your eyes out," old Marusha cried, and sprang up like a maddened cat between the Cossack and the young woman, and stretched out towards him her two bony hands.

She wanted to say something more, to utter some prayer and entreaty, but suddenly a blow rang out, and old Marusha crumbled to the ground like a bag of broken bones and groaned: "Have mercy, Father."

The Cossack stretched out his hand and tried to seize Deborah, but with the agility of a cat, she sprang aside. Her eyes sought for help, and there flashed before her the soft form of the young Cossack, lighted up by the fire where he stood. His sad, velvet glance seemed to caress her, and a sudden hope of salvation flashed up in her mind.

"Save me from him, I don't want to belong to him," she said, and clung to the young Cossack, seeking shelter near him, as does a child under a tree when it rains.

The young Cossack quivered. Her girlish voice, which he heard for the first time, since he had captured her, made his heart leap, and when she looked into his face with her moist prayerful eyes, he was unable to bear her glance, and avoided it. He remained standing firm as a tree, and did not stir. His face became pale and his heart began to beat strangely.

For a minute the second Cossack looked to see

what the young man would do, then with heavy steps
he approached the girl and stretched out his hand
towards her.

"He cheated in the game, I will not go to him,"
Deborah cried, when the Cossack began to approach
her.

The young man was still standing mute and motionless as a tree. But in his eyes a little fire had lighted
up.

"Be silent, accursed one, and come to your master."
He tried to seize Deborah by the hand and drag her
to himself.

The young Cossack moved swiftly to one side and
placed himself directly opposite the other.

Two knife-blades flashed up in the light of the fire.

"Cossacks, what are you doing?   Will you slaughter
one another for a Jew girl? Are there not enough
Jew girls in Ukraine? Cossacks, reflect what you
are doing," the third one shouted.

But he was afraid to approach. Both Cossacks
stood facing each other, looking into each other's eyes,
and the curved Turkish knives glistened in the light.

And suddenly, like a wild animal, the young one
leaped upon the other with his knife, and the next
moment the older man lay on the ground and rattled
heavily in the night.

"Curses on you, you sinful soul! For the sake of
a Jew girl you have murdered a Cossack, may the
sin lie upon you like a heavy burden wherever you
turn and wherever you go," the second old man

cursed.   Then he spat out and walked off by himself
into the night.

For a moment the young man stood and seemed
lost in thought.   Then he appeared to remember
something and called after the retreating Cossack into
the night.

"Ho there old man, where are you going?"

"I will not have anything to do with you, you have
sold your soul to the devil," a voice replied to him
from the blackness of the night.

For a minute he stood still, not knowing what to
do.   He looked about him, seeking the girl with his
eyes.   He found her lying on the grass unconscious.

He stooped, lifted her up and brought her to the
fire.   Then he took his cloak and covered her.   He
sat down near her alone.   The light of the fire illumined her face.   He saw how white her face was, and
the lids which were drawn over her eyes as in a dove,
and a tender feeling took possession of him for the
frail creature that lay near him.

CHAPTER TEN

IN THE OPEN FIELD

"What is your name, Jew girl?" the Cossack asked.

"Deborah."

"And mine is Yerem," the tall Cossack flashed his white teeth in a smile.

Deborah shivered.

"Why do you shiver? Are you cold, Jew girl?"

Deborah nodded.

"Come closer to the fire."

But Deborah remembered the nurse and looked around for her.

"What are you looking for, the old woman?" asked the Cossack. And he took up old Marusha, who lay motionless on the ground from the blow she had received, and dragged her over to Deborah. Deborah seized her old head and pressed it to her bosom.

"Wait, now, I'll make her well again," said Yerem. "Hey, old woman, take a pull out of this horn," and the Cossack put to her mouth the horn of spirits which he carried with him. "Take a good drink, you can afford yourself, the little brothers have enough."

After drinking Marusha opened her eyes, looked about her, and seeing Deborah near her, embraced her eagerly.

"You are alive, my little bird! Thank God!"
And approaching Yerem on all fours, she seized his
hands and kissed them.

"You eagle, you mighty one who saved us from the
hands of the Evil One, save us, in God's name, save
the little bird. Oh, you angel sent by God!"

"And what is she to you, a daughter?"

"More than a daughter, my all, my life, my soul,"
and she embraced Deborah as if wishing to shield
her.

"But she is Jewish and you are a Christian."

"I don't know myself. She is knitted to my soul,
though of a different faith, like a bird from a strange
nest. Haven't I brought her up from childhood?
Her and her husband, from the time when they were
still tiny ones."

"She has a husband?"

"Yes, eagle, married not long ago. Came back
from the school, got married, settled down in their
nest—to hatch little ones—and just then came the
misfortune."

"And where are her people?"

"God alone knows. Saved themselves or fell into
the hands of the Cossacks. Who knows if they are
alive?"

"How could they be alive, being lost among the
Cossacks?" he declared, and approaching Deborah,
he took her hand and asked:

"And are you willing to be mine, Jew girl?"
Deborah was silent.

"How yours, eagle? Hasn't she a husband?" said old Marusha.

"Be silent, old woman, her people are not living any more. The Cossacks have killed all the Jews, so she has no more husband. If you will be mine, Jew girl, you will live, if not, you will die. Just as you like."

Deborah remained silent.

"Well, why don't you answer, Jew girl? It will be a bad thing if you don't answer. By right, you belonged to Yefrem Skvoz. He won you with the dice. But he cheated, so I killed him and saved you. For myself I have saved you. Because you please me and I took a liking to you as soon as I saw you. Well, now, say, Jew girl, are you willing to be mine? You promised, didn't you?"

Deborah was still silent.

"But you are so good, you are an angel. A mother bore you, not a bitch, like those others. There is God in your heart. How can you do such a thing? You will not commit a sin before God. She has a husband," Marusha pleaded.

"Be silent, old woman, or I'll beat you up as Yefrem did. You have been told, haven't you, that her husband is not living any more? He's been killed, all the Jews have been killed."

"But suppose he has saved himself?" asks the old woman.

"He's been killed, and if not, then I'll kill him. And you, old woman, be silent, you devil. You are a Cossack woman, and you should side with the

Cossack, not with the Jew.   You have sold your soul
to the Jew devil; beware, old woman!" said the Cossack
angrily.   He then sat down at the fire near Deborah,
took her hand and said to her as gently as he could:

"You belong to me; from the very first I saw
that you were young and beautiful.   Through the
rags in which the old woman dressed you, I saw all
that.   And the moment I looked at you my heart
leaped, and at once I loved you and had pity for you
as for a little fledgeling dove.   To no one will I give
you up, neither to the Hetman nor the Khan.   I will
kill them all and keep you for myself."

For a minute Deborah was silent.   Suddenly she
looked straight into the Cossack's eyes and said:

"I am in your hands and you can do with me what
you please, and yet I am not afraid of you.   One
stronger than you keeps guard over me.   You may
beat me and I am not afraid of you.   Should I wish
to, I will be fond, and should I not wish to, I will
not be fond."

"'Should I wish to I will be fond, and should I not
wish to I will not be fond'—well said, Jew girl, well
said.   And I will not force you to be fond of me.
But if you will not, this is what I will do," says the
Cossack, and approaches the old woman.   "I don't
know what she is to you, a mother or something else.
It is all the same.   Come, now, Jew girl, if you will
be mine, I'll let her live, if not I'll kill her."

Deborah's eyes flashed.   Only for a moment was
she in doubt.   Then it became clear to her that she

must save the old woman. How to save her she did not yet know, though she was ready for anything.

Then she said with an appearance of bashfulness:

"Your wife I will be, but not your mistress."

"That is right; there you have spoken well. That suits me: my wife you will be, but not my mistress."

"What have you done, daughter? For the sake of my old days you have sinned before God. What have you done?" Marusha exclaimed.

"Be silent, old woman. Do I not love her?" said the Cossack, deeply moved. "It can be nothing else, but she has cast a spell over me. My best comrade I have killed for her. He was my uncle," he pointed to the dead Cossack, "my teacher he was, taught me to ride and shoot and I have killed him for a Jew girl. My own mother I could kill for her. It's nothing else but a spell that she has cast over me."

A sudden thought occurred to Deborah. She stood up from near the fire, and drawing herself up to her full height in the light of the flame, she remained standing like an apparition from another world.

"It was I who brought that about."

"How did you bring it about?"

"With the magic which I possess."

"And broke the oath which you swore to your husband, and forgot God, you wretched creature!" the old woman reviled her.

Deborah raised her thin, beautiful arms to the sky, and threw back her pallid face to the stars.

"So I have been ordered to do."

"By whom?"

"By Him who dwells on high, and through His might."

The simple Cossack was frightened at her expression. He turned to the nurse:

"What is she saying?"

"I do not know," the nurse also stammered with fear. "I do not recognize her. It's with her God that she speaks in that way."

"My body I have anointed with the magic ointment which He gave me, and no one can do me any harm. Here I stand before you, now try your knife on me and see if I lie."

The Cossack was terrified. His nostrils began to tremble and his knife twitched in his hand.

"What are you doing? What are you saying?" the nurse embraced her.

"You fool, oh you old fool! Why are you frightened? Do you not know that when God protects me no harm can come to me?"

The nurse sank down on her knees before her, seized her hands and buried in them her old face which was wet with tears.

The Cossack stood at a distance, trembling. A terror had taken possession of the tall, strong peasant in the presence of the girl.

"Come home to my mother, Jew girl. In my mother's house I will keep you until the wedding. The Cossacks may come and see you and take you away from me."

"I will not go with you until you have sworn me an oath by your soul and by your faith."

"I will swear for you any oath, beautiful Jew girl. Say what you wish me to swear to you by my soul and my faith."

"I know, Yerem, that you are good. You have saved me from wicked hands. You have not permitted evil to befall me. God will reward you for all that. Promise me now, Yerem, before I go with you, that until the wedding you will spare me, respect my purity and do me no evil."

The tall Cossack smiled.

"Before God I promise you, my beautiful Jew girl, that until the wedding I will spare you, respect your purity and do you no evil."

"Remember, Yerem, you have promised by your faith and sworn by your soul. And if you will have evil thoughts and desire to do me evil, then through the magic which I possess I will at once know your thoughts. And as soon as you will desire to do me evil, the Higher Power which protects me will come at once and take me away from you. And you will not be able to help it."

"Before God I swear," says the trembling Cossack, "to guard you like a holy ikon, like a saint." And he wrapped her up in his long white Cossack cloak and led her out of the field to his mother's home. Old Marusha followed them. And the dawn began to pale, lighting up the tops of the trees, which began to look out upon the world as out of a mist.

CHAPTER ELEVEN

For the Faith and for the Torah

Chmelnitzki continued to negotiate with the Polish Field Marshall Dominick with regard to submitting to the Polish Crown, and at the same time continued to send his Cossack hordes to destroy defenseless towns in order to pay his Cossacks with the loot. To maintain the friendship of the Tatars he had to enrich the harems of the Khan with beautiful young Jewesses. A horde of ten thousand Cossacks, led by one of his brigands named Krivonos, fell upon the cities and towns of Ukrainia and wiped them off the face of the earth. The Cossack hordes were followed by bands of Tatars like swarms of black birds of prey.

In vain did the noble Prince Vishnewetzki beg the Polish nobles and authorities for help for this little army of Polish soldiers who fought against the Cossacks and Tatars. His voice which warned against the Cossack danger remained unheeded. The Field Marshall Dominick still counted on Chmelnitzki's justice and willingness to submit to Poland. He continued to make concessions to the Cossacks, and to confer new honors and titles on Chmelnitzki, thinking in this manner to placate the Cossack leader. The nobles were engrossed in the election of a new king to succeed king Vladislav who had died. No

one was concerned over the fate of the distant Uk-
rainian province. In the end Vishnewetzki himself
had to leave his little army and travel to Warsaw
to seek help from the dissolute nobles for the unhappy
people of Ukrainia.

In the meantime the entire region lay defenseless
and open to the Cossack hordes. Like a river which
overflows its banks, they overran one city after
another, annihilating all living things. They plund-
ered and burnt the cities; and the people, young and
old, Polish and Jewish, they put to the sword. Only
those who were suitable for the slave-markets, the
Tatars allowed to live. And they enriched their harems with the comely women and girls.

After Nemirov they headed for Tulchin. In the
fortress of Tulchin the Jews from the surrounding
towns as well as the fugitives from Nemirov had
taken refuge. So there was assembled in Tulchin a
Jewish population of ten thousand souls and considerable wealth which the Jews had taken with them.
The Cossacks headed for this wealth, and the Tatars
for the women and the girls.

But Krivonos and his hordes of Cossacks found it
no easy matter to capture Tulchin. The city was
fortified, and the Jews who were, for the most part,
fugitives from towns that had been destroyed, knew
what it meant to fall into the hands of the Cossacks.
So they determined, rather than fall into the
Cossacks' hands, to starve to death in the city or die
in battle.

In the city there were also quite a number of Poles

and several hundred Polish soldiers. So the Jews and
the Poles entered into a solemn pact under oath, and
the rabbi, Reb Aaron, the head of the Tulchin yeshivah and the Duke Tchwerchinski affixed their signat-
ures to a document. They agreed to fight side by
side to the last man and the last drop of blood in
defense of the city against the Cossacks.

And a great friendship rose up between the Poles
and the Jews. The Jews gathered in the synagogues,
the Poles in the churches, and prayed God to save
them from the hands of the Cossacks, and they swore
to defend each other. They called each other comrade. The Poles addressed the Jews as "dear
friends," and the Jews shared with them the food
which they brought together in the city to enable them
to withstand the siege until help should come from
the Polish nobles.

The Poles and the Polish soldiers commanded by
Duke Tchwerchinski, who were more familiar with
the art of warfare than the Jews, and knew how to
use firearms, undertook to defend the fort of Tulchin.
And the Jews, who were more numerous and more
courageous than the Poles, being in greater danger,
undertook to defend the weaker and less defensible
sections of the city.

They armed themselves with Turkish weapons and
flint-locks, which they obtained from the fort.
Around the rampart they raised high scaffolds and
ladders, built platforms, and assembled heaps of
stones and other heavy objects. The women prepared great cauldrons of molten tallow, scalding

cereals and boiling water, and brought them to the ramparts. Frequently the Jews allowed the Cossacks to come close to the wall and apply their crowbars for making a breach. Then the Jews would suddenly hurl down upon them a hail of rocks and pour down on their heads cauldrons of seething tallow. And the Cossacks fled, leaving behind them their crowbars together with their dead at the foot of the walls. And more than once did the Jews, as in ancient times during the siege of Jerusalem, sally forth out of the city, and with utter contempt of death, they fell upon the ranks of the Cossacks, killed many of them and drove the rest back to their tents.

The food-supply of the city, however, began to dwindle. The food which the Jews had gathered in the city was, by a special food administration, divided into two equal parts for the Jews and the Poles. First they fed the women and children. The men would frequently capture their food from the Cossacks. By their sentinels they were informed of the time when the Cossacks used to drive together herds of sheep and other cattle, and the Jews would rush out of the city and into the midst of the Cossacks, take away the cattle and drive them into the city. In this way the Jews would provide the city with food enough to last for weeks.

Among the Jewish defenders was Mendel, the parnas of Zlochov. After losing his son under his very eyes as he swam across the river, and hearing nothing of his daughter-in-law, who had gone away with old Marusha, he took his wife and went with her to Tulchin, together with other fugitives, in the hope that old Marusha might have brought Deborah to Tulchin by a different road. But not finding her in Tulchin and being certain that his son, after falling into the hands of the Cossacks, was no longer alive, he grew tired of life. Having nothing further to live for, he had no further desire to live. But Mendel's instincts were too robust, and his fear of God too strong, for him to put an end to himself. He, like many others, having lost all hopes of personal happiness, gave up all his thoughts to the welfare of the community as a whole. The community of Tulchin became his child, his Shlomo, his future, his own life. In the community he found his strength again, and for its life he threw himself into battle with an utter contempt of death, and of the personal happiness of which he felt the need no longer. Wishing to die for the Jewish faith, he was the first to throw himself into battle, first in dangerous enterprises, inspiring the others to follow him, kindling a holy enthusiasm in them with his words.

"Jews," he would say, his eyes sparkling with inspiration, "they have killed our children, they will kill us, but our God lives forever. Then let us battle for His glory, for the faith and for the Torah."

And the Cossacks no longer understood or recognized the Jews. Are those the Jews who used to gather in the towns like bound sheep, like slaughtered fowl? Like wild tigers the Jews used to rush out upon the Cossacks from the ramparts, with bare hands or armed with clubs or crowbars, and with the cry

"For the faith and for the Torah," they fell upon
the hordes of Cossacks. They paid no heed to the
arrows which fell among them nor to the bullets, nor
could they be halted by the roar of the cannon.
With cries and blazing eyes, they tore through the
clouds of smoke which belched from the mouths of
the cannon, and fell upon the Cossacks, bit them with
their teeth, gouged out their eyes with their fingers,
and with their long knives they slashed throats and
cleaved heads. Often a Jew would clasp a Cossack
in a furious embrace, bury his teeth into the Cossack's
throat, and with characteristic Jewish stubbornness
hang on until they fell down together, and Jewish
and Christian blood mingled on the ground.

Many Jews, in their readiness to die, put on burial-
clothes, prayer-robes and prayer-shawls, and with
knives in their hands, rushed in among the Cossacks.
The hordes, seeing the white-clad figures sweeping
through the night with blazing eyes and faces illumined by a holy light, were stricken with panic. They
used to sink down on their knees before the white Jews
and pray to them as to angels:

"Lord, have mercy!"

Others were stricken with terror by the dreadful
anger which blazed from the white Jewish faces, and
they fled with wild cries as though pursued by un-
earthly apparitions and spread panic among the Cossacks. And whole regiments of soldiers fled before
the Jews dressed in their burial-dress, leaving everything behind them.

For weeks the Cossack army lay encamped behind

the walls of Tulchin, unable to take the city. In vain did Krivonos curse and revile his captains, the Cossacks fled before the white Jews as if the terror of God had struck them. Krivonos, however, had determined to take the city by storm. He was ashamed before the Tatars in his camp that the Cossacks were running away from the Jews. He was afraid of Chmelnitzki and feared also lest the Khan of the Tatars become aware of the matter. So he gathered together great hosts of Cossacks and peasants from all the surrounding regions. In their tens of thousands came the peasants from the towns and villages. Horses, vehicles and men covered the country roads about Tulchin as with a black garment. In the city could be heard the roaring and neighing that rose up from the camps of the besiegers. At night their blazing fires could be seen over the entire steppe, myriads of fires stretching far, far across the steppe.

The Jews were not afraid, being ready to die to the last man. Not like sheep would they die, however, but in battle, in battle for God and for His Torah. The slogan which the parnas of Zlochov had proclaimed in the community, transformed men doomed to death into heroes, rekindled in the Jews the ancient Jewish spirit. Death was a joy to them. And as in olden times behind the gates of Jerusalem, so did they fight now. All night the women carried stones up the ladders, boiled tallow and lead, and dragged large buckets of pitch upon the scaffolds behind the walls, making ready for the battle.

Tchwerchinski and his six hundred Polish soldiers, armed with muskets and cannon, were in the fort. With him, also, was the entire Polish population of Tulchin, and all were armed to defend the city.

When the first glint of dawn lighted the summits of the towers of Tulchin, Krivonos ordered his first ranks to the wall with iron borers. These consisted of peasants from the surrounding region, whom Krivonos had armed. He expected that the Jews would hurl down upon them all their stones and pour out all their pitch, so that when the more experienced Cossack soldiers approached, the Jews would be weakened. But unexpectedly the Jews let fly with cannon before the peasants arrived at the wall. In the night they had removed the cannon from the fort and stationed them on buildings near the wall. When the peasants heard the roar of the cannon and found themselves enveloped in clouds of smoke, they fled in every direction. Krivonos ordered out column after column, and the Jews continued to drive them off with bullets and cannonballs. All day the Jews kept on driving the Cossacks away from the walls, but when night came the Cossacks finally reached the wall and began to place their borers in position. Then the Jews met them with a hail of stones, poured upon them molten lead and heated cereals; lumps of burning pitch fell from the wall on the heads of the Cossacks. Many were burned by the flames and lay smoldering across their borers. But ever greater numbers of Cossacks continued to gallop up to the wall on their horses, and the fire which rained down from the walls consumed them in ever greater numbers.

The Cossacks bellowed and shouted and roared, urging each other on with shouts and hurrahs, but the rain of fire did not cease from the rampart and the heaps of corpses smoldering in the burning pitch rose ever higher at the foot of the wall. Finally the gate of the wall opened and hosts of white Jews rushed out; and with knives in their hands, and the cry "For God and for His Torah," they fell upon the hordes like demons. And as soon as the peasants saw the white hosts of Jews, the terror of God fell upon them and they fled in every direction. And the Jews returned to the city singing Psalms.

Night came at last, and the Cossacks gathered around their campfires. From the other side of the wall the singing could still be heard. All night the sound of singing was heard from the city. It was the song of those who sang Psalms and cried aloud to God. And it was not the cry of such as are besieged, but a great paean of praise from those who are prepared to die for His glory, for the faith and for the Torah.

And in the starry night the Cossacks whispered to each other, seated near their fires:

"The ancient Jewish God has awakened, has come back from Jerusalem, and is now with the Jews in the city. Woe unto us! Woe unto us!"

CHAPTER TWELVE

The Letter

In his tent, on a pile of Cossack rugs, lay Krivonos, the Cossack leader, covered with a sheep-skin coat, although it was a warm night in the month of Ab. The atmosphere of the tent was heavy with a stifling odor of a kind of horse-tallow with which an old Cossack granny, half sorceress and half healer, anointed the legs of the leader every night. The odor of the tallow gripped the throat and irritated the nose. The Cossack officers who sat around the leader set up such a violent sneezing and coughing that the flames of the tallow candles which were stuck in the tall Turkish candle-sticks writhed and flickered.

Krivonos was in very bad humor. He was tortured by the rheumatism. His legs and feet were moist, and felt as heavy as if big stones were tied to them. And the tent was so hot, and inside his legs was a sharp pain which gnawed and gnawed like a worm, and made it impossible to think of anything else. And there were such important and serious matters to consider. It was now four weeks that they had been besieging Tulchin, unable to take the city. They should long ago have been in Bar, they should have been in Lvov, and Prince Vishnewetzki might arrive in the meantime. And all because of what? Because of the Jews! It was not soldiers who were holding them up, but Jews! How would such a thing appear to Chmelnitzki? Unable to take Tulchin because of the Jews! Cossacks fleeing before Jews! He cursed and reviled his captains, and the nearest one whom he was able to reach he struck a violent blow on the head with his club.

"Oh you boobies, clods! Since when have Cossacks been running before Jews? The Tatars will learn of it, the Khan will scoff at us, will laugh in his sleeve. We'll become a mockery and a byword. Then he will desert the Cossacks and go back to Astrakhan, and the little brothers will be left alone, a plaything for the Poles to be taken to Warsaw and there beheaded."

"Ah, dear little father, do not scold. Of the Jews alone we would have no fear. It's the Demon we are afraid of, the Demon who has begun to hobnob with the Jews. As soon as the Jews come out of the gates, the Demon appears among them. He is dressed in white robes and has long knives in his hands. And the Demon is so numerous, the devil knows what it all means. Now he is here, now he is there. And the moment the Cossacks spy the Demon among the Jews, nothing will avail. They throw everything away and run, so that you couldn't hold them with iron chains."

"It's not the Demon, it's their God who appears in the robes," says another captain. "It is said that their God has returned and is aiding them. In that case, woe unto us Cossacks!"

"God or Demon, you, captains, deserve to be be-

headed for the disgrace which you have brought on
the Cossacks.   We have promised the Khan two
hundred girls and women from Tulchin, besides many
slaves.   And here we stand, and the Jews even take
away our cattle.   Was such a thing ever heard of?
Are you Cossacks?   Dogs, that's what you are, mangy
curs, women's petticoats!''   the leader cursed and
struck at those whom he could reach.

"Ah, dear little brother, you'll not accomplish
anything here.   We must devise a trick, some clever
trick for getting into the city, just as we did in Nemirov.   There is nothing else to do,'' says one of them.

"You'll not fool them any more with Polish flags.
Nemirov has made the Jew devils crafty.''

In a corner sat a silent Cossack, a tall thin fellow,
with calm black eyes, who observed all things closely
and said nothing.   Though his face was rough and
savage, he nevertheless had the appearance of one
who was "literate,'' a "scholar'' among the Cossacks.
He had a melancholy expression and was busy
picking lice from under his arms.

"Hey, you! Why are you silent?   What are you
scheming?   You hear everything and say nothing,''
the chief flung at the silent Cossack.

"What is there to say?   There is nothing to say,
we must act,'' replied the Cossack without interrupt-
ing his occupation which, it was evident from his
expression, afforded him immense pleasure.

"And how shall we act?''
"Write a letter.''

"To whom? To the Jews?" they all asked in surprise.

"Be silent, Cossacks!" the chief commands.

"To the Pollacks."

"What shall we write to them?" asks the chief.

"We must remind them of our Lord Jesus. Hiding behind Jews, that's what they are doing! How is it they are not ashamed of themselves? It's a disgrace for a Christian to seek protection from a Jew. Let them deliver the Jews to us, and we will spare them like Christians and divide the booty between us."

"What? Let our enemy the Pollack live, so that he may avenge himself on the Cossack later?"

"And deliver the booty to them?"

"Who ever heard of Cossacks asking Pollacks for favors?"

"Let them but open the gates of the city, let us but find ourselves inside the city, then we shall see," the Cossack replies.

"Ah, Vassil, you old fox."

"And what will happen if the Pollack will not listen to us?"

"We must write in such a way that he *will* listen. There is no more bread in the city. Soon, the food will give out completely, and then, when they fall into the hands of the Cossacks——"

"Good!"

"Sit down, scribe, and write. I will dictate," the chief commanded.

The tall Cossack, who was the counsellor, and the only "literate" one among the Cossacks, sat down at the table, which was covered with little pools of brandy and littered with the leavings of the last meal. He cleaned the table and threw over it a Cossack cloak. Then he took out of a little box a piece of parchment, a goose-quill and ink of a sort, which he had taken along for the purpose. They moved the candle-sticks closer to him, and the Cossacks sat or stood around him, helping to dictate the letter to the Poles.

But Krivonos found it impossible to give any thought to the letter. The pain in his legs became sharper and more biting. His face which scowled with anger took on a grimace of pain, and he shouted:

"The granny! Bring in the granny!"

One of the Cossacks went out and returned a few minutes later with the old woman.

"Blood is what we need, fresh blood of a young thing,—and it must be still warm so that it may warm up your bones, dear little father, and the pain will stop," said the granny, feeling the Cossack's suffering limbs.

The Cossack became silent. They looked at each other with earnest, thoughtful faces, on which a sort of fear was discernible. More than once had they seen in Nemirov and other cities the fresh blood of young, still palpitating, little bodies that had been rent asunder. But they themselves did not do it. It was the Tatars who did it. The Cossacks did not murder children, only older people.

"How do you mean, fresh blood—Jewish?" asked the chief.

"The blood of a kid will do," the old woman replied.

"Go, dear little son, bring me a kid, a young one. There must be such a one in the stables. If not, go to the fold and bring me a little lamb, but it must be young, newly born," the old woman explained to one of the Cossacks.

The Cossack went out and after a long while returned, holding in his arms a white little kid which looked around in surprise, frightened by the lights and the people, and cried in a quavering voice like a little child.

"Rend it apart, dear little father, and let the blood flow on your sick legs," said the old woman to Krivonos, "Then cover your legs with the torn little body, and the pain will subside at once."

Krivonos stretched out his bare sick legs and took the little kid. The creature trembled. Its quavering call ended abruptly. Then a stream of young, fresh, warm blood began to flow down on the Cossack's legs, which he then covered with the warm lacerated flesh.

"And now cover yourself well, dear little father, and let the blood warm you through. You have given Satan his due, he will now calm himself."

And, in truth, the Cossack leader now felt his pain relieved. The young, fresh, still palpitating little body yielded a pleasant warmth like the body of an infant. The pain disappeared and Krivonos was able to dictate the letter:

"In the name of Jesus Christ, may He be glorified for ever and ever, Amen!

"Before our worthy brothers, the Poles, we beat

the ground with our foreheads, and send you greetings. We pray for you day and night to our Lord God that He preserve you against war, famine and pestilence, to-day and forever, Amen!

"It has come to our ears how the name of our Lord God is become a mockery and a byword, and we have seen how Christians, our worthy brothers, the Poles, are put to shame in that they seek protection and safety from the enemies of Christ, the Jews. Wherefore our Christian hearts have been exceedingly pained. Is it fair and fitting that Christians, our worthy brothers the Poles, should enter into comradeship with the enemies of Christ, the Jews, against their brother Christians? And is it fair and fitting that the valorous Poles should allow themselves to be protected by Jews? Wherefore we have thought to send you messengers with greetings and peace, and we pray you, dear brothers, to receive well our messengers and fittingly, and to give ear to their words.

"Dear brothers!

"Not against you nor your wives and children, nor against your possessions, nor against anything which is yours have the Cossacks gone out to wage war. Not against Christians do we wage war, but against the enemies of Christ, against the Jews who crucified our Lord Jesus, and stole our possessions. Against them and against everything which is theirs have the Cossacks gone out to fight the battle of Christ. You, Poles, are our brothers, and we will treat you like brothers. If you will deliver the Jews to us, then we will spare you and your wives and children and everything which belongs to you. And in order that the Jews may not hide away their possessions, proclaim among them that we, the Cossacks, are prepared to abandon the city if they will assemble all their possessions, their gold and silver, their silks and garments, and offer them as a ransom. Let the Jews bring their wealth to you in the fort, and when they shall have brought together their gold and silver, open for us the gates of the fort and let the Cossacks in. On the enemies of Christ we will avenge ourselves even as they did crucify God. But you and your wives and children and everything which is yours we will spare, and the wealth we will share with you. So help us our Lord Jesus Christ, Amen!"

In the dark night two riders took the parchment, which was written with the aid of the warm blood of the rent kid, to the Christians of Tulchin. A white flag fluttered pale in the light of the stars. And when the sentinels on the tower of the fort called down to the horsemen: "Who goes there?" the horsemen raised aloft their white flag and the parchment and called out:

"In the name of Jesus Christ."

CHAPTER THIRTEEN

The Great Ordeal

Duke Tchwerchinski informed the Jews that the Cossacks were ready to abandon the city in return for all the gold and silver, the silk fur-coats, and other garments which the Jews would offer as a ransom. Reb Aaron, the head of the yeshivah and rabbi of the city, called a meeting of the parnasim and notables, and they resolved to redeem their lives with their possessions. So they proclaimed in the synagogues, in the market-places and about the ramparts that the Jews bring all their belongings to the Duke in the castle as ransom for the Cossacks.

And the Jews assembled their possessions, saying to themselves: "Let gold and silver be the scape-goat for our lives," and praised God who sends salvation.

There were many precious vessels among the objects which the Jews brought to the castle: silver-filigree cups, the work of the Nuremberg craftsmen, which the Jews had brought from the fairs; lime-boxes in the shape of various fruits; spice-rods shaped like towers and engraved with flags and the signs of the zodiac, and menorahs with the symbols of the tribes. There were also all manner of jewels, of gold and silver and precious stones; expensive fur coats of sable and mink which they had bought from the Russian merchants;

and much cloth of silk for garments, Italian brocades which they had purchased for ark-curtains and bridal gifts, and silks from Slutzk inwoven with silver and gold. For they withheld nothing in order to redeem their lives. And they assembled all this wealth in great heaps in the fort of Tulchin. The broad silver neck-bands gleamed among the dark, heavy furs, and the gold jewels and precious stones sparkled among the wave of silks, velvets and satins which lay in heaps in the court-yards of the castle ready for the Cossacks.

And as soon as the Jews had brought all their wealth the Duke said:

"Give up your arms and bring them to this place."

Whereupon the Jews said:

"What need has the Cossack of our arms? He has arms enough, and well he knows that we shall not pursue him when he withdraws from here. And we have taken up our arms only in order to defend ourselves and not, God forfend, for the purpose of attacking him. And now, since he is withdrawing from here and wishes to wage war against us no longer, what need has he of our arms?"

To which the Duke replied:

"The Cossack demands it, and he and I have so agreed."

Then the Jews realized that the Poles had made a compact with the Cossacks for destroying them.

And Mendel, the parnas of Zlochov, spoke and said:

"We have brought you our wealth, but our arms we will not deliver up. For, if you demand our arms, it can mean nothing else than that you have made a compact with the Cossacks to betray us and deliver us into their hands. For what else can it mean that you demand from us the weapons with which we defended and saved the city?"

And other Jews spoke after the parnas and said:

"We will give up our wealth, but we will not surrender our arms."

And still other Jews cried aloud and answered the Duke:

"If we must die, then let us all die, the Poles together with the Jews!"

And there was a young man there from Karsoon; he was thin and tall and his eyes blazed with the vengeance of God. His ear-locks trembled and the teeth in his jaws chattered with anger, for the wrath of the Lord burned strong within him. And he snatched up a long knife and cried to the Jews:

"The gentiles have betrayed us here just as in Nemirov. Let us avenge ourselves on them with the vengeance of the Lord, for God and for His Torah!"

Like a sudden burst of flames the words of the young man seized upon the excited assembly. They had nothing more to lose. They had long before made their peace with death, but they wished to sell their lives dearly. There suddenly kindled up within them the ancient Jewish wrath. Their eyes blazed, earlocks trembled and teeth gnashed. Weapons appeared in their hands and a rumbling as of distant thunder passed through the multitude:

"The Gentiles have sold us!"

"For Nemirov!"

"For innocent Jewish blood!"

"For the faith and for the Torah!"

And the multitudes, young men and old, two thousand strong, with the long knives in their hands, began to close in on the Poles, and soon the Duke with his soldiers and the other Poles together with their wives and children, all of whom were in the fort, were surrounded by the infuriated Jewish throng. The Jews drew nearer and nearer, forming a circle with the Poles in the center. Some of the Jews were already rushing on the Poles with their knives, and in another moment the most frightful massacre would have taken place, for the Jews were exceedingly exasperated. Suddenly some one in the throng called out:

"Jews! Children of Israel, ye merciful sons of the merciful, what are you doing?"

The multitude halted, and from its midst came forth an old man with a small beard of lustrous whiteness. He was dressed all in white, and with his bare, bony arms, which extended from his prayer-robe, he held back the enraged people.

"Woe unto the eyes that look upon this!" the old man cried. "Are these the merciful sons of the merciful? How can you forget yourselves just before your death, before the coming of the great ordeal!"

The people halted in the presence of the white beard, the bare arms and the long prayer-robe. They lowered their knives and there was a silence in the

multitude as in a synagogue before the blowing of
the *shofar*.

"Jews are responsible one for another!" the old
man cried aloud. "If you kill the Gentiles they will
avenge themselves on the Jews of other cities. Jews
must not harbor any wrath, we must not take any
revenge in our behalf! Save your strength for the
proper moment when the great ordeal will arrive, for
kiddush ha-shem, for the faith and for the Torah!"

"They have sold us to the Cossacks! They will
murder us as they did in Nemirov!" one of the people
cried.

"And why are you better than the Jews of Nemirov?
Did they not die for the sanctification of His Name?
The Lord of the Universe calls for our souls, we will
render them unto Him with joy and gladness. And
let our hands be clean. We will not be like the Gentiles. They have betrayed us. May God's wrath
for the blood of the Jews which flows like water, fall
upon their heads. We will not profane with revenge
the *kiddush ha-shem* which God requires of us. We
must look on and be silent—such is the will of God.
Jews, give up your arms! If the Lord of the Universe
wishes to help us, do we need our arms, those bits of
wood and iron? Does the Omnipotent—He in the palm
of whose hand are heaven and earth—does He need
human weapons in order to help us? That is the
salvation of the Gentiles. That is their strength.
Our strength is God, and therefore save your own
strength for Him, for the faith and for the Torah,
when the great ordeal will come!"

Then one stepped out from the multitude, approached the Polish nobleman who, with the other Poles, stood and trembled in presence of the strange storm which raged around them, and threw his arms at his feet.

And one after another they stepped up to the nobleman and threw at his feet their earthly weapons.

A smile of bliss irradiated their features, their eyes blazed with a holy light. With a profound inner happiness, which transfigured their faces, they threw their weapons at the feet of the hobleman without raising their heads or giving him a glance, for they were so engrossed in their inner bliss that they were unconscious of his presence.

The duke gave a command and the Poles opened the gate. The Jews said not a word. And soon the Polish soldiers surrounded them and ordered them to move on. The Jews started off. Rabbis in prayer-shawls walked in advance and the rest followed. And then the entire multitude, men, women, and children, took up jubilantly the song which the cantors were singing:

> The Lord is my light and my salvation,
> Whom shall I fear?
> The Lord is the stronghold of my life,
> Of whom shall I be afraid?

And with song on their lips, they went forth to meet their death.

CHAPTER FOURTEEN

KIDDUSH HA-SHEM

Nay, but for Thy sake are we killed all the day.
(Psalms)

The Cossacks waited outside the fort. They surrounded the Jews and began to corral them like sheep, driving them into a large orchard with a fence around it. About two thousand Jews were there, men, women, and children. Among them were several rabbis: the old rabbi, Reb Aaron, the head of the yeshivah of Tulchin, and other rabbis, who were great students of the kabbalah. And they, together with the devout little tailor, who was already dressed in his burial-clothes with his prayer-shawl thrown over his head, were leading the Jews. The cantors continued to sing so as to prevent the Jews from falling into melancholy and being stricken, God forfend, with weakness. And the multitude sang after them:

> Though a host should encamp against me,
> My heart shall not fear;
> Though war should rise up against me,
> Even then will I be confident.

The Jews did not know what the Cossacks intended to do with them: to let them live or to massacre them. It was all one to them. A courage which passed all understanding inspired them to die. They saw the gates of paradise opening before them. And it was not death they feared, but lest they be separated, lest their wives and children be taken from them. With their own hands they were ready to kill their nearest and dearest rather than see them defiled. The women looked upon the men, and in their glance was the knowledge of death. They did not weep, not even the children wept. The singing of the cantors transported them into such an exaltation, into such spiritual joy, that every earthly feeling fell away from them, and some of them already lived the serene and infinite life of the beyond.

The orchard was full of ripe fruit. It was the month of Ellul, and the sun was shining, and the world had a holiday aspect, and they were all together, and the cantors were singing. And some of them saw a blue light, with the sky opening to receive them, and already they floated through the infinite space. And some heard the song which flows from the world beyond, where God sits with the righteous and expounds to them the Torah. And the children thought a great, great *Yom Kippur* had come, that the great Teacher Moses was about to arrive, that King David would play on his harp, and another moment and Messiah the King would come galloping on his white steed. There he comes galloping right out of the clouds, and everybody is waiting for him, and the next moment he will be here descending from the clouds.

And fear was transformed into joy. A profound, infinite joy united them all. Fathers, mothers and children came together, and the whole multitude be-

came as one family. The men held each other by
their girdles, the children clung to their mothers, and
the entire community gathered close about their
rabbis and cantors. And the spirit of festiveness
became exceedingly great, and, no one knows how, but
one of the multitude suddenly began to chant the
Praise Service:

> Hallelujah.
> Praise ye the name of the Lord;
> Give praise, O ye servants of the Lord...

The cantors took up the Praise Service, and sang
the verses of the Psalms in the holiday tune. The
Praise Service roused the Jews to such a pitch of
enthusiasm that they all caught up the tune, and the
entire community, men, women and children, made
the orchard ring with the festive song:

> From the rising of the sun unto the going
>   down thereof
> The Lord's name is to be praised.
> The Lord is high above all nations,
> His glory is above the heavens.
> Who is like unto the Lord our God,
> That is enthroned on high?

And the Jews took no note of how the orchard became filled with Cossacks and Tatars. Some of the
newcomers were half naked, their bodies bulging out,
in their hands nail-studded clubs. Others carried
crooked swords, and the Tatars, through their small,
half-closed eyes, peered at the women and girls and

children. The Jews saw no one. They were all
huddled together like a flock of sheep in a storm, the
women and children in the center, and around them
the men holding each other by the girdles.

> Out of my straits I called upon the Lord;
> He answered me with great enlargement.
> The Lord is for me, I will not fear;
> What can man do unto me?
> The Lord is for me as my helper;
> And I shall gaze upon them that hate me!

A sound of trumpets was heard in the orchard.
The Cossacks shouted hurrah, and made way for a
a Cossack of small stature. On that hot Ellul day
he wore a long fur cloak and a fur hat with a large
tuft of feathers. The sun was hot and the long fur
cloak trailed behind him. A Greek Catholic priest
in a silk skirt walked behind him, holding aloft a
large cross. A choir of church-singers, headed by one
carrying a banner with a sacred image graven upon
it, followed the priest. The Jews saw neither the
Cossack leader Krivonos nor the church procession.
They closed their eyes so as not to see the cross and
the sacred Christian image, and raised their voices
louder as they sang the Psalms:

> All nations compass me about;
> Verily, in the name of the Lord I will cut
> them off.
> They compass me about, yea, they compass
> me about;

Verily, in the name of the Lord I will cut
   them off.
They compass me about like bees;
They are quenched as the fire of thorns;
Verily, in the name of the Lord I will cut
   them off.

The Jewish voices mingled with the church choir,
and it was as though the murderer and his victim were
together intoning to God a song of praise in the glorious
sunlight. The church choir soon became silent. The
priest took the banner with the sacred image and
stuck the pole into the earth. On a green knoll near
the banner the small, sickly Cossack who was per-
spiring in the long fur cloak, took his stand. Krivonos' face was gloomy and impassive like the face of
a sick man. For a minute he gazed upon the compact
Jewish multitude holding each other's hands, their
song swelling louder and louder with ever greater joy
and ecstasy, seeing neither him nor the sacred image
nor the Cossacks standing around them with swords,
pikes and clubs, as though they were somewhere else,
seeing other things and hearing other voices, and
knowing nothing of what was going on around them.

Krivonos was frightened by the tempestuous singing
of the Jews. He was frightened by the ecstasy which
shone in their faces, and remained standing in bewilderment, not knowing what to do. His sickly
face became agitated and his little eyes opened wide
with an expression of fear. The priest handed him
the cross.

Krivonos did not know what to do with the cross. He looked with fear, now at the Cossacks, now at the Jews.   At length he lifted the cross high above his head, and, with that gesture, his self-assurance came back to him.

"Jews!" he cried, "Whoever will come near the flag and bow down before the cross shall live!"

The Jews did not hear his words.   They did not even see him who stood there and spoke to them. None of them glanced even once at Krivonos or the Cossacks.   Again their voices resounded joyously among the trees and mounted into the brilliant sky:

> The voice of rejoicing and salvation is in the
>   tents of the righteous;
> The right hand of the Lord doeth valiantly.

"Jews, I call on you again!   Do you not hear me? He who wishes to live, let him come to the flag and bow down before the cross!"

> The right hand of the Lord is exalted;
> The right hand of the Lord doeth valiantly.

The song of the Jews rang out louder and more resonant in the orchard.

Krivonos stood bewildered and did not know what to do.   He looked in perplexity at the priest.

"It's Satan whom they are sending against you. Drive him off and do the work of God," said the priest to the trembling Krivonos, and made over him the sign of the cross three times.

"For the last time I call upon you: Whoever will
accept the Christian faith shall live. Come here to the
cross!"

> This is the day which the Lord hath made;
> We will rejoice and be glad in it.
> This is the day which the Lord hath made;
> We will rejoice and be glad in it.

This was the reply the Jews made in joyous song.

And again Krivonos remained standing, not knowing
what to do, and looked with bewilderment at the priest.

"Do the work of God," said the priest, again and
again making the sign of the cross over him.

"Cossacks! The Jews! At them! Hurrah!"

The shout of "Hurrah!" rang through the orchard,
and from every nook of it Cossacks rushed out upon
the Jews. Some carried crooked swords, others long
pikes, still others nail-studded clubs. And they fell
upon the Jews.

The Jews embraced each other, husbands, wives and
children clasped in each other's arms, and they
cried in unison:

"Hear, O Israel, the Lord our God, the Lord is One!"

For a moment the cry to God seemed to rise above
the shouting of the Cossacks. But one by one they
were silenced, snuffed out like the flames of candles.
And amid the trampled grass and broken branches
were stretched out whole families: fathers, mothers,
and children. Their blood became intermingled and
their souls rose up together. They died clasped in

each other's arms together intoning the "Shema Yisroel!"

Fourteen hundred men, women and children were slaughtered that day in that orchard of Tulchin by the Cossacks. The rest were led away by the Tatars to the slave-markets. But not a single one of them purchased his life with his faith.

———

Under a tree, in the trampled grass and amid broken branches, lay the body of the parnas of Zlochov. His eyes were open and turned heaven-ward. Even now, with all the pallor of its lips, his face, which had aged considerably in the past few months, revealed strength and vitality, and it was hard to believe that the tanned face with the rough, peeling skin was dead. For there shone on the face the most tranquil and wholesome of smiles.

And perhaps the reason for that was that near him lay Yocheved. But how her face looked can not be known, because she kept it buried in his bosom...

The orchard was as silent as the steppe. In the grass and amid broken branches, trampled fruit and dry leaves, bodies lay strewn, trampled and crushed like the fruits of the trees. One might think there lay only bundles of garments bespattered with mud and blood. Only where a face appeared, either of a man with blood-clotted ear-locks, or of a woman with dove-like eyes sealed, or of a sleeping child, there shone forth the calm, demure smile of a profound inner bliss. It was as though the people lived on, and saw something in their new life, and heard something, not of this world and not of this earth.

———

On the green knoll the Christian flag fluttered as though ashamed. Krivonos had forgotten to take it with him when he went into the city to massacre the Christian Polish population.

CHAPTER FIFTEEN

In the Orchard

All day the orchard of Yerem's mother was fragrant with honey. The bees buzzed in and out of the bee-hives, which were built in hollow trees, and swarmed about the white, sun-bathed honey flowers with which the entire field of the orchard was covered. The branches of the trees sagged under the loads of ripe plums which kept falling to the ground. They were left there to rot in the grass and emitted the sharp odor of decaying fruit. Several sheep wandered about the orchard with long black wool and stupefied expressions, who seemed to bore themselves with nibbling the grass and, out of boredom, licked each other with their long tongues. A swarm of little ducks arrived on the scene together, like a deputation of respectable housewives on an important mission, swaying their fat little bodies on their short legs. For no reason at all, a goose suddenly flapped in, its wings spread out awkwardly, and started off with a great outcry; but suddenly coming upon the dog Bugo, whom she woke up from his sleep, she reeled back in great fear, and in order to avoid unpleasant developments, she went off in another direction, folded her wings, and finally calmed herself.

In the orchard, among the sheep, the ducks, the geese and other domestic birds and beasts, Deborah wandered about.   On her feet she wore little shackles, which Yerem had placed there in order to prevent her from escaping, and that he might always hear her footsteps.   And instead of her own headdress, she already wore a Cossack veil on her head, which concealed her face.   She roamed listlessly about the gardden, and the bells rang mournfully in time to her slow footsteps.   And in this manner, she came to the brook, which ran through the orchard, and sitting down on the bank, gazed into the water.

But Yerem, who watched her footsteps, followed her.   Slowly he came up to the brook, and sat down near her.

"Why are you still sad, pretty Jew girl?   You are still unable to forget your people.   You have cast a spell over me and you have poisoned my heart.   Woe is me, what will I do?"

"Be silent, Yerem, you have promised me, have you not, that until the wedding you will not torment me, and will let me bewail my people?"

"Yes, that is true; true, I did promise you.   But my heart becomes as withered as a parched spring only from looking at you.   And you refuse to eat our bread.   You insult our food and eat only what your nurse brings you,—fruits and vegetables.   And you are already my bride, are you not?"

"I promised my dead, Yerem, to observe their law until I shall leave them.   Oh Yerem, let me observe my law.   For you are good, and you love me."

"Yes, my love for you is terrible, Deborah.   Because of you I shall die very young.   I will commit crimes for you. I could kill my own brother for you. Say it, and I will go with you to the end of the world. We will settle on a lonely island, a little brook will run in front of our house and red poppies will blossom before our windows. And I will be your peasant and you will be my queen. Oh! Queen mine, little angel mine, you pure dove, what is this power that you have? Your eyes are like those of a dove, and they are breaking my heart and I could die here, on this spot."

The young peasant bowed before her and, burying his face in his hands, he suddenly broke into sobbing like a little child.

"Calm yourself, Yerem. You are good, and I like you. Your heart is good. Calm yourself, Yerem." And she stroked his hair with her hand as a mistress strokes her dog.

"Oh, you white little lamb of mine, Oh, you dove mine, why do you torment me so, my love? Why do you torture my heart so? Oh, make an end of my life altogether."

"Oh, you will live, Yerem, you are young and strong and you are good."

"But of what good is my life to me, if I do not know when you will be mine? You lay it off from day to day, and love gnaws at my heart as the worm at the tree, and I am withering away. Tell me, my angel, where will I build my house? Near what river and in what land?"

"Oh, Yerem, you will not have to wait long, not much longer," she said sadly.

"Tell me when?"

"You promised me faithfully that you will not torment me, for you love me."

"Good, I am silent now. If you wish it, say it;
if not, tug away at my soul, tug away at my heart.
Let it gnaw and gnaw until I die." And the peasant
dug his face into the grass.

"Soon now the end will come, only wait a little,
Yerem. It will be soon now, it will be soon." She
calmed him by laying her cool, white hand on his head,
and her burning eyes sought some place in the distance.

He watched over her like the apple of his eye, and
followed her footsteps like a faithful slave. The
Cossacks and peasants made a laughing stock of him,
taunted him for sticking to his Jew girl, and a rumor
began to circulate that the Jew girl had cast a spell
over him: it could mean nothing else.

One day Yerem returned from the city and brought
something for Deborah.

"All the Jews and Poles of Tulchin have been killed,
not a single one has been left alive," he told her.

"How do you know, Yerem?" Deborah asked him.

"The peasants in the city reported it. They
brought there a great many articles, which they had
taken from the Jews, and here I have brought you
something also, my pretty Jew girl. I bought it from
a peasant for you. I gave him a sheepskin coat for
it."

And Yerem took out of a shawl a pair of golden
slippers and gave them to her.

"They say that the Jews buy such slippers for their

brides and that the Jew girls like very much to wear them, so I bought them for you, my pretty Jew girl."

Deborah took the slippers and examined them. She recognized them. They were the slippers which Shlomo had brought her from Lublin when he came home from the yeshivah.

"How did you come by them?" Deborah asked him.

"Bought them from a peasant. He found them on a dead Jew whom they had killed in Tulchin. The Jew held them clasped to his heart."

"Was he a young man, that Jew, or an old one?" Deborah asked him.

"I do not know, my pretty Jew girl. He did not tell me. But why have you become so pale, my little dove?"

"Afterwards, afterwards, I will tell you. The nurse, I want the nurse!"

"What ails you? Why are you so pale, little angel mine, dovelet mine? Why?" The young peasant asked amazed.

"Afterwards, I will tell you everything. Oh, Yerem, soon, very soon, will be my wedding. Only for these slippers have I waited. Now the end will come soon. Nurse!"

"Nurse!" Yerem called.

And the old nurse barely had time to run out of the orchard, where she was feeding the chickens, when Deborah fell down on the lawn.

"What ails her?" the peasant asked the nurse.

The nurse saw the slippers in Deborah's hands and uttered a great cry:

"Lord, have mercy!" and caught up Deborah in her arms.

Yerem stood by in amazement.

CHAPTER SIXTEEN

THE GOLDEN SLIPPERS

The same evening the little, white honey flowers opened their petals and the garden was sweet with the fragrance of honey. Fireflies flashed and flickered in the air like souls astray. Far out on the steppe, little fires darted up here and there and died away. Each red poppy-head flared up. The stars huddled close together and the air shone with a supernatural light as though it were full of invisible bodies come floating out of another world.

Deborah stood in the orchard near the bonfire which Yerem had lighted. From the hut came the strumming of a "lyre" which a stray "ancient" was playing, as he sang a ballad to the assembled peasants. Drunken cries, weeping and laughter, also came from the hut where the peasants had collected all the loot which they had stolen from the Jews of Tulchin. They were dividing this loot and drinking Jewish wine. And the old man played for them on the lyre.

Deborah stood near the fire, the shackles on her ankles ringing with every move she made. She stood like a young sapling, her eyes turned toward the stars. And she spoke as if she saw some one:

"Soon I shall come to you, my husband, my chosen one. I see you in the light. Your arms are stretched

out to me.   Take me to yourself, my husband, my
chosen one.   I long for you."

She saw a blue sea flooded with light, and star-
studded boats floating about.   They are all sailing
to the same shore.   It is so light there.   Impossible
to look into the light.   What a great light is there!
The infinite, the everlasting is there!   God is there,
and all are floating straight into the great light.   In
every boat there is a Jewish family.   She knows them
all, all who are in the boats.   And she seeks among the
boats.   And now she sees him.   He is waiting for her
in his boat.   The others have all floated away.   He
alone is waiting.   And now she calls to him:

"Shlomo, Shlomo, wait for me.   I come, I come,
I come."   And she stretched out her arms towards
the little boat in the sky.

"Whom do you see?   Whom are you speaking to?
What ails you, beautiful Jew girl?"

"Do not touch me.   I am fire, you'll catch fire
from me.   See I am burning.   I am a torch and you
will burn yourself!"

Her eyes blazed and her face caught the light of
the shimmering stars.   Her supple young form, draped
in light colored shawls, seemed to have been kindled
in the flames of the fire.   She appeared to be burning.

Yerem looked at Deborah and did not recognize
her.   It seemed to him that he had once seen her
somewhere, but he could not remember where.   Then
something like a great light rose up before him.

"I know you!   I know who you are!   Oh, I know,
sinful soul that I am!   Oh! Oh!"   And he sank to

his knees before Deborah and began to pray as one
prays before a holy ikon.

"Oh, Lord, have mercy!" And he buried his face
in his hands and began to weep.

"I know. Now, I know. I have recognized you.
You are a holy one, you are a saint. I saw you in
church. On the holy ikon I saw you. Oh, I know
now, sinful soul that I am. Have mercy, have mercy"!
the peasant stammered.

"Be not afraid, Yerem. You are good. You have
a good heart. Be not afraid."

"Oh, sinful soul that I am! Have mercy." And
the young peasant jumped up and ran away from her.
And with a great noise he entered the hut where the
peasants were assembled.

"Peasants," he cried, "God is in the orchard, woe
unto us!"

The peasants put away their wine. The lyre became silent. They turned pale and asked each other:

"What is he saying?"

But Yerem was frightened and wept like a little
child. He pointed to the orchard.

"There, outside!"

The peasants became infected with his dread.
Stealthily and in great awe they approached the door
of the hut and looked out.

"Where?"

"There, near the fire. Don't you see? Look! Look!"

"Your Jew girl is standing there, not God."

"I've recognized her. She came down from the
ikon. It is God!"

"She has cast a spell over you, she has bewitched you. Don't you see it's your Jew girl, not God? Do not sin."

"Peasants, I've recognized her. I looked deep into her face and recognized her. She is a saint. She has come down from the holy ikon."

"Let her prove that she is God."

"A miracle!"

"Let her perform a miracle and we'll believe that she is God. If not, then your accursed Jew girl is a witch. Then she ought to be burned."

"She has bewitched the lad. Into the fire with her!"

"Peasants, be silent and do not sin," Yerem exclaimed; and approaching Deborah, he knelt before her from a distance and made obeisance before her as before a holy ikon.

"Tell them, show them that I am not mistaken. Let them believe in God. Oh, prove to them, holy one, prove to them that you are God."

For a long interval Deborah was silent. Then she turned her luminous face to Yerem and said:

"Call the nurse, Yerem."

But the nurse had been near her for a long time. She lay at her feet, her face hidden in Deborah's dress, and wept.

"Go, nurse, and bring me the golden slippers," said Deborah in Yiddish.

"Oh, my child, my little dove, I can not. What are you going to do?"

"I command you, nurse. Bring me the golden slippers."

The nurse went to her room and brought the golden slippers.

"Do not weep. Be merry. Put the slippers on me as you used to do when I was a little child. Do you remember how you sent me to him once when he was a little boy with a pear and an apple?" She whispered to the nurse.

"Oh, I understand, I understand. But what are you going to do?"

"Why, I am going to him. He is waiting there for me in his little boat to sail away with me to heaven." And she embraced the nurse and kissed her.

The nurse withdrew from her, and Deborah, the golden slippers on her feet, said to the trembling Yerem:

"Yerem, take your flint-lock and fire at me."

A dread fell upon the peasants. They became infected with the panic which possessed Yerem. Deborah's words terrified them. Some began to believe that they were in the presence of something supernatural. And one of them sank to his knees and mumbled:

"Lord, have mercy!"

And Yerem trembled and shook with fear.

"No, no, I'll not do it. I am afraid."

"Be not afraid, Yerem, no harm can come to me. I am not here any more. I am already there, in heaven. I have put on the golden slippers which he sent me from heaven so that I might come to him. Go, Yerem, take your flint-lock and aim at my heart."

But the peasant continued to sob, and he stammered:

"No, no, I am afraid, have mercy."

"I command you, Yerem. Go and bring the flint-lock, I will stand here near the fire so that you can see where to aim. Have I not told you that no harm can come to me? I command you. Do as I have said."

Illumined by the flames of the fire, she looked like a young goddess who commands. And the fear of God fell upon the peasants. They sank to their knees. One of them began to chant and the rest joined him:

"Lord, have mercy! Lord, have mercy!"

One of the peasants handed the flint-lock to the kneeling Yerem. Deborah in the golden slippers stood in the light of the fire.

"Shoot, Yerem!"

The peasants became silent. They remained kneeling on the ground.

A report was heard. A little cloud of smoke rose up and caught the light of the fire.

"Aim well, Yerem. See, no harm can come to me."

Yerem discharged the weapon a second time. And again a little cloud of smoke rose into the air.

Deborah began to sway and to sink to her knees.

"She falls!"

"Blood!"

"The accursed Jew girl! She has cheated us!" the peasants shouted, rising to their feet and running towards Deborah with clenched fists.

"Accursed Jew girl! Cheated us!"

But Yerem now stood guard over her. He held in his arms her swaying body, from which the blood flowed into the flames of the fire.

"Why have you done it, beautiful Jew girl? I loved you so?" He stammered.

"Forgive me, Yerem, forgive me. I thank you for sending me to him. I knew you would send me to him. You are good, Yerem."

"Give her to me, she is my child!" cried the nurse, and running up she caught Deborah in her arms.

Deborah now saw the star-studded boat. Shlomo was taking her by the hand to help her embark.

"Farewell, nurse," she stammered.

"A happy journey, my child," the nurse replied in Yiddish.

And as though wanting to be alone, Deborah withdrew from Yerem, turned away from the nurse. She laid her head on the grass and the peasants who surrounded her heard from her lips the words which in those days they heard so often from the Jews:

"Hear, O Israel, the Lord our God, the Lord is One!"

And she became silent.

In the city of Lublin, on the occasion of the annual fair, there came together that year the Assembly of the Four Countries. A great task lay before the Assembly. A great many Jews from the whole of Ukraine had congregated in Lublin. Fathers came seeking their children who had been carried off by the Cossacks, and many women were there who did not know whether they were wives or widows. And men were there whose wives had been carried off by the Tatars, and fatherless orphans and Jews whose settlements had been destroyed and who had roamed all over the country unable to find a resting place.

The city was full of refugees. Many found their kin whom they had long believed dead. Fathers found their children, husbands their wives, brothers their sisters. The Assembly strove to reconstruct Jewish life, to re-unite the families which the Cossacks and Tatars had cut asunder. It issued a decree commanding all Jews from the towns which had been destroyed to return and rebuild the Jewish communities, for the Polish king with his armies had driven the Cossacks back to the Russians, and Chmelnitzki was a captive in the hands of the Tatars. The Assembly collected a ransom fund from the wealthy and sent it to Turkey for the ransom of the Jewish captives. It granted permission to husbands to take back, for the sake of the children, the wives who had been held in captivity by the Cossacks. And it received back into Judaism those whom the Cossacks had compelled to embrace a strange faith.

Among the refugees was Shlomele also. He had been ransomed by the Turkish Jews, together with other captives of the Tatars, who had brought him to the slave market at Constantinople. The Jews of Turkey learned that Shlomele was a graduate of the famous yeshivah of Lublin, so they wanted him to stay in Turkey, where they thought to open a yeshivah for the study of the Talmud in the Polish manner by the method of *pilpul*. But Shlomo longed greatly for his own people in Poland. So a Jewish merchant of Saloniki took him aboard his vessel, which was bound with a cargo of merchandise for Naples. In Italy, also, they sought to detain him that he might teach young men the Talmud in the Polish manner. But Shlomo insisted on going home to Poland. So the Italian rabbis, some of them his comrades who had studied with him in the yeshivah of Lublin, gave him money and clothes and sent him away to Germany.

For a long time he wandered about in Germany. There the terrible news reached him of what the Cossacks had done to the Jews of Tulchin, of Bar, and of the other towns. Finally he came to Poland and hastened to the fair in Lublin in the hope of getting some news of his own kin.

In Lublin he came upon refugees from Tulchin, from Bar and from other towns, and he learned from some of the forced converts of the death of his father and mother, who had died for the sanctification of His Name together with the other Jews of Tulchin. But no one knew what had become of Deborah—of Deborah or of the Christian nurse.

But Shlomo knew. He knew that she had gone up to heaven in holiness and purity. In heaven she was, and waiting for him.

He did not mourn for her. Only a great longing for her took possession of him, and for the day when he would again be with her.

And he roamed about through the fair of Lublin among the refugees, among the husbands separated from their wives and the wives separated from their husbands, among the widows and the orphans. He heard the signs and moans of his people which rose up over the fair. And he pondered deeply on the matter. He sought to understand the meaning of it all. For a minute the meaning escaped him,—he could not understand, and he fell in a state of melancholy. And this caused him deep grief, for it is a matter of common knowledge that melancholy is only one degree removed from doubting.

And one day he walked in a narrow street in Lublin where the merchants' stalls were located. And he saw standing before an empty booth an old man who was calling buyers into his booth. And he marvelled greatly, for the booth was empty, there was nothing in it to sell. And he walked into the booth and asked the old man:

"What do you sell here? Your booth is void and empty, and there is no merchandise in it."

And the old man answered:

"I sell faith."

And he looked intently at the old man, and the old man appeared to him familiar as though he had seen him before....

THE END